MAID AT MUIRFIELD

When Hannah Miller loses her servant's position, she is glad to quickly find another at Muirfield Hall. There she discovers that she is filling the shoes of Ellen, a maid who drowned in the lake under suspicious circumstances. Soon Hannah is drawn into playing detective, as it turns out that Ellen knew many secrets about the Muirfield staff. Handsome gardener Adam also catches her eye; but his taciturn nature and love of plants, which Hannah doesn't share, are thorns in her side. Are they destined to be together?

CAROL MacLEAN

MAID AT MUIRFIELD

Complete and Unabridged

LINFORD
Leicester

First published in Great Britain in 2017

First Linford Edition
published 2018

A catalogue record for this book is available
from the British Library.

ISBN 978–1–4448–3654–7

Published by
F. A. Thorpe (Publishing)
Anstey, Leicestershire

Set by Words & Graphics Ltd.
Anstey, Leicestershire
Printed and bound in Great Britain by
T. J. International Ltd., Padstow, Cornwall

This book is printed on acid-free paper

1

A New Job

I tramped across the fields, the stubble of harvested crops hard under my thin-soled boots and the hems of my skirts damp and stained with soil. It bothered me not one bit because the air was so sweet and sharp. The sun shone as brightly as if it was the height of summer, and a flock of birds skimmed by like tiny shadows in the sky. And there it was, ahead of me. The cottage, nestling low amongst the heather and moor grasses, its whitewashed walls gleaming and beckoning me on.

I caught my breath. I still did not have my full strength back after the illness. Nevertheless, I swung my bags and hummed a tune as I walked the last stretch of beaten path home. I knocked once, hard, on the wooden door; then, not waiting, I pushed it open.

A familiar smell of peat smoke and vegetable stew wafted up. The room was dark, and it was difficult to make out the figures inside. The cottage windows were tiny and the ceiling low-beamed, designed so as to keep in the heat. A person rose from the fire and came towards me. She grabbed me and gave me a fierce hug, then set me from her with a frown.

'Hannah, what are you doing home? What's wrong?'

I wanted to curl into her arms like I had when I was small. Let my mother take away my worries and protect me. But here I was, a grown woman nearly twenty years of age, so it wouldn't do at all. Besides, her expression mixed concern with rising anger.

'Mrs Collington let me go. Can I come inside?'

She drew me in, taking my bags, and shut the door against the cold day. As my eyes adjusted to the low light, I saw that nothing had changed. There was the fireplace, a log burning nicely and a couple of peat sods leaking grey smoke. The flagged stones of the floor were scrubbed clean. The furniture was simple, a solid oak table and four chairs and mam's special dresser with its good pieces of blue and white china proudly displayed. They'd been a gift from her employer. She'd worked most of her life for one local family of gentry until she'd given it up to get married to my father.

Kitty was grinning at me from her seat at the table. A mound of clothes was in front of her, and her needle flashed as she sewed quick and neat on a white blouse.

'If you've been sacked, you can come and help me with this lot. Grab a seat and a dish of pins.'

'Give your sister a moment,' Mam said, and turning back to me, pushed out a chair. 'Sit down and I'll bring you a cup of tea. You look peaky.'

'Where's Dad?' I wanted to see him immediately.

She shook her head wearily. 'He's asleep. You can go through later.'

They waited until I had drunk half a cup of strongly brewed tea and eaten a soft round of farl before insisting on hearing why I was back. Part of me kept listening for any sound from the next room. I longed for my dad. I'd missed him terribly.

'What did you do wrong?' Mam asked sharply. 'You must've done something.'

'No, no, that's not it at all,' I protested. 'Mr and Mrs Collington were very pleased with me. They said I looked after little Arthur very well. He's a lovely boy, very nicely mannered, and with such a sense of mischief.'

'Well, what then?' Mam said. 'If you were doing so well, why let you go? You've worked there for two good years. I thought you had a place there until young Arthur went to school.'

'There was influenza in the house. It started with the footman; he'd been visiting his family in Glasgow and

4

brought it back with him. We all came down with it like flies. Only it's lingered with me. I couldn't shake it off. Then Mrs Collington said she was very sorry but she couldn't have her servants looking after me and having to get someone in for Arthur too. She said I had to go.'

'Are you better?' Kitty asked, laying a gentle hand on mine with concern.

'I'm better now, but it's too late. They got a new girl in, one of the housemaid's cousins, to do my job.' I squeezed her fingers affectionately. Kitty was a couple of years younger than me. She'd been born with one leg shorter than the other, which meant she was lame, and so she hadn't gone into service the way I had. She helped Mam instead.

'You can't stay here,' Mam said, her voice rising. 'We can barely feed ourselves as it is. Kitty and I take in washing and sewing from the big houses around, but it's hardly enough. If only your father . . . '

She pushed herself up from the table and stared at the fire, rubbing her arms as if she was frozen. I noticed she was thinner. Kitty too, her face more angular, her rounded cheeks no longer apparent.

All had been well until a year ago, when Dad had had an accident. He was employed as a farm labourer for Home Farm. A piece of machinery had crushed his arm, and now he couldn't work. It was up to Mam, Kitty and me to make the money that kept us all from the workhouse. Living in at the Collingtons' had helped. I had my board and lodgings, my uniforms and my meals, plus a wage that was not too shabby.

'You'll have to go tomorrow to the Servant's Registry,' Mam was saying now, more to herself than to me. 'Perhaps they will be able to find you a place quickly.'

'The nearest Registry is in Glasgow, is it not?' I asked her. I wondered how she thought I was going to get to the city. I supposed I could walk back over the fields and get a lift, if I was lucky, on a farmer's cart, and then get myself somehow to the railway station. It would be a long journey.

'Oh no, she won't have to do that,' Kitty piped up with a big smile on her face. 'I happen to know that they're looking for a maid up at Muirfield Hall.'

Mam frowned at her, a deep groove like a black line, between her eyebrows. 'And where, missy, did you hear of that?'

'Muirfield Hall?' I chimed in. I hadn't heard of the place.

Kitty's chin went up and she puffed with the pride of knowing all the answers. Answers her mam and her big sister clearly had not!

'Brigid, who brings the washing, she said they needed a girl up at the Hall. She asked me if I knew anyone who needed a place.'

'Brigid O'Connell, is that?' Mam asked, still with that groove deep furrowed in her forehead.

I wished she didn't need to worry so much. I wished . . . oh well, wishes weren't going to do any of us any good. Life was hard, that much was true. It was only hard grind and determination that put food on the table.

'Aye, Brigid O'Connell.' Kitty nodded. 'Biddy's daughter. Said she'd give it a go herself, if she didn't fear her mammy so much. Biddy won't let her give up her position at the Manor. She gets such a fair wage there and they're good to her. She gets every second Sunday off and she gets out of the house to bring the mending here.'

'Ah, well,' my mam sighed. She said no more.

In the silence, I asked again, 'Where is Muirfield Hall? I don't know it at all.'

'It's a county over, that's why,' Kitty said. 'That's the downside — you won't be visiting us much.'

'I haven't got the job yet,' I teased.

Kitty rolled her eyes.

Mam stared hard at me. 'You'd better get it. There's no place for you here.

I'm sorry, Hannah, but that's the way it is.'

'So what do I do?' I asked Kitty. I felt odd, taking the advice of my younger sister. Kitty had always looked up to me. I was older by two years and whole in body. I'd taken care of her when we were children, made sure she didn't fall into a ditch or trip on her poor leg. Now, it seemed, she was the boss of me.

'Well, the way Brigid put it, whoever wants the job, Mr Dawton will come personally and interview them. If they are suitable, like, he'll take them back that very day in his carriage to Muirfield Hall.'

Mama and I both looked at her. Kitty modestly dipped her head and began to sew once more.

There was a creak of bedsprings in the next room. I leapt up and ran through. Dad was awake. He lay in the wrinkled bed sheets, his chest rising and falling with shallow breaths.

'Hannah, my darling girl.' He reached for me with a shaking hand.

I grasped it and pulled myself close to hug him. I loved my mother, but I adored my father. It was thinking of him and how proud he was of me that got me through each day of employment.

'Are you an apparition?' he wheezed.

'No, it's me, Dad. Really me.' I leaned in and stroked his cheek. I felt the prickle of his beard and saw with dismay how grey his whiskers were. He was getting old.

'You're home for good?'

I shook my head sadly. 'No, just stopping by for a few days, that's all.'

'A pity. I wish you could come back. I remember when you were but a little lass, the songs we sang and the games we played. If only time stood still — or better yet, if time went backwards. You and Kitty, small again and safe with me. And I'd be strong, a full man. Not a cripple like you see me now.'

'Oh, Dad,' I cried, and hugged him tightly.

'Never mind, lass. Never mind. Tell me, are you well? You're a bit pale around the gills.'

So I told him all of what had happened at the Colllingtons' house, and he was angry and indignant on my behalf. But it couldn't change the fact that I'd lost my job.

Later, he managed to get out of bed and make it through to the table. Kitty had set it for four. Mam served up hot vegetable stew and bread fresh from the skillet. I ate hungrily, my appetite returning after the long weeks when I'd had none. Kitty polished off her portion quickly and asked for more. Mam and Dad took smaller portions but said they were satisfied with what they had. It was so lovely to be home with my family around me. I had no idea what the future held for me. I wanted only to hold on to this moment and treasure it.

* * *

In the end, the interview lasted no more than five minutes. Mr Dawton pronounced himself satisfied with me, and before I knew it, I was sitting in the carriage with my luggage at my feet and the horses were clip-clopping me away from all that I knew. He seemed a vague sort of gentleman, my new employer. As if his thoughts were far away inside his head. Certainly he hadn't asked me much. I think that once he saw I was clean, well turned out and could speak nicely, that was enough. I wondered what Mrs Dawton wanted in her new maid and whether I'd pass muster.

So I stared out of the carriage window as the landscape passed by. It was early autumn, and the fields were all golden brown and full of geese and small brown birds feasting. The low swell of the hills was purple with the heather, backlit with a streaky sky. The journey was long enough that my toes were chilled when I finally stepped down from the vehicle.

Mr Dawton had directed his driver to drop me at the side of the house so that I could use the servants' entrance at the back. I watched as the carriage disappeared. Then, stamping my feet to get the blood flowing in my toes, I glanced about.

It was not what I'd expected. I'd thought to find Muirfield Hall a bleak sort of place deep in the moors. In fact, the house was set amongst woodlands, and I glimpsed the tall walls of a large garden at the side of it. Beyond the woods, the inevitable moor and marsh began to take over, stretching then to the low hills on the skyline.

I went inside. It wasn't a large country residence, so it was not surprising to me that there were only a few people bustling about. A girl in a maid's uniform smiled at me.

'Are you the new kitchen maid, then?'

'Kitchen maid?' I said in dismay. 'I was told it was a housemaid's position.' The truth was that being a kitchen maid was drudgery compared to being a housemaid, and even that was terrible hard work.

'I'm Gracie,' the girl said with another shy smile. 'I'll tell Mrs Smith you're here. She's the housekeeper and will let you know your duties.'

Mrs Smith appeared and beckoned me into a room. It was plainly decorated but warm and cosy, and I realised this was her own sitting room as befitted her station. She was a small woman, not as tall as me, but she had an air of authority. Her keys rattled as she sat, and indicated that I should too.

'Welcome to Muirfield,' she said. 'You and I will have no cross words between us as long as you work hard here. You will be helping in the house and in the kitchen with Cook. Now, Gracie will find you a uniform and you can get started.'

I opened and shut my mouth. I had questions. I was curious about this new place. But Mrs Smith had risen and was going out of the door. My impression of her was that she was efficient but not unkind.

Gracie found me and pointed to a cupboard where I was to fetch my maid's clothes. 'Ellen was taller than you, but you can take up the hems. Or there's Mary's dress and apron; they might fit you better.'

'Where are Ellen and Mary?' I asked, lifting down a neat pile of dark dresses and snowy white aprons.

'Oh, you don't know then?'

'Know what?' I frowned at her. I draped one of the dresses against me, measuring its length to my ankles. I wished Kitty was here. She was far better a seamstress than I.

'It's Ellen's position you're filling,' Gracie said. 'She drowned. And I suppose you're filling Mary's position, too. She was the maid before Ellen, but she died of a fever last year.'

I hastily put down Mary's dress. I didn't want to catch anything.

Gracie laughed and picked it up again. 'Don't be afraid; these are all laundered and steamed and just ready to wear. Come along and I'll show you where you'll sleep. You're in with me.'

I wasn't sure I liked the idea that two previous maids had died for me to be here. Still, Gracie didn't seem bothered, so why should I be? These things happened. A little shiver ran up my spine till I pushed my unease aside.

I was so busy trying to peek into all the rooms that I bumped into a solid chest. 'I'm so sorry,' I said, looking up in embarrassment.

A tall, solemn young man with sandy hair stood there. 'It's only Bill.' Gracie smiled. 'He won't mind you trying to knock him down, will you, Bill?'

'You must be Hannah,' he said. 'I hope you'll be happy here.' It didn't sound like he had high hopes that would be so.

I nodded, and then Gracie was pulling me away, impatient to show me the servants' quarters.

'He's a bit miserable,' I commented.

Gracie just shook her head. 'He's all right, is Bill. Got a lot on his plate, that's all.'

I wanted to ask what he did have on his plate, but decided that was too nosey for a newcomer.

16

The maids' rooms were at the top of the house, three storeys up. The top floor was clearly used only for the servants, as no one had bothered very much with the decor. The floors were bare wood with a thin skim of polish. The walls were a dull cream colour, no fancy wallpapers or prettiness. It was chilly too. I supposed there weren't many fires lit up here.

'Here we are,' Gracie said with pride, pushing open a brown door. 'You'll be sharing with me.'

It was a narrow room with two iron-framed beds, each with a bedside cabinet. One bed had a wooden kist at the end of it, draped with a small square of embroidered linen. I put my luggage at the foot of the other. It wasn't too bad. Not as nice as the room I'd had at the Collingtons', which I didn't have to share, but it would do.

'Where do the other maids sleep?' I asked.

'There's just you and me up here, apart from Sarah, who's next door.

Cook's room is further along the corridor. Janet is the scullery maid and she sleeps downstairs in the kitchen. Which doesn't sound good, but is a whole lot warmer than up here in the winter. Bill is the footman, and the men's quarters are the other side of the house from us. It's a small staff here. Muirfield Hall isn't very large or fancy, despite what Mrs Dawton would have everyone believe. She'd rather be in Glasgow, but Mr Dawton won't leave here because of the gardens.'

I followed Gracie's nod and looked out of the window. We were very high up here and I got a good view. Now I could see the tops of the trees and right into part of the walled garden. There were greenhouses along one side and lots of strange colourful plants that I'd never seen before. We were at the back of the house. There was a stables, and further out a row of cottages and more glass houses. Beyond that I made out a large lake and what looked like a summerhouse.

'Is that where Ellen had her accident?' I asked.

Gracie stood beside me at the window. Now she turned with a surprised expression.

'Where she drowned?' I prompted, when no answer came.

'Ellen drowned all right. But it wasn't an accident. She was murdered.'

2

Meeting Adam

'Murdered?' Surely I hadn't heard her right.

Gracie nodded. She looked scared. 'It's been horrible. They sent a detective all the way from Glasgow. A big man with a cape. He questioned everyone and took lots of notes, but he didn't find the murderer.'

'When did . . . ?' I couldn't bring myself to say 'murder'. 'When did it happen?'

'Just a few weeks ago.' Gracie sat on my bed. 'We've been managing without Ellen since then, and I'm very glad you're here. There's too much work for me on my own.'

'What does Sarah do?'

'Oh, Sarah's too fancy to help in the house.' Gracie wrinkled her nose. 'No, she's lady's maid to Mrs Dawton and the two young ladies.'

'What are they like?' I sat beside her on the bed, hearing the springs creak.

'Alice is sixteen and thinks herself quite grown up and grand, but she's a silly sort of girl. Emily is twelve. I feel a bit sorry for her in spite of her being from a good family. She drifts about looking lost most of the time.' Gracie leapt up suddenly. 'Goodness, we mustn't sit here gossiping. Mrs Smith will have our guts for garters.'

'Just one more thing,' I said, unable to leave it alone. 'How did they know Ellen was murdered? Surely she might just as easily have slipped and fallen into the lake?'

'There were signs of a scuffle in the mud at the edge of the lake, near to the summerhouse. They reckon she must've sneaked out at night to meet someone. They found her body the next morning.' Gracie shuddered. 'She was my friend, you know. I've had awful nightmares ever since. I might wake you

21

up at night with them. I scream and all sorts.'

She waited while I put on my new uniform. I hitched up the skirts at the waist, as they were too long, and promised myself to sew the hems that night.

I couldn't put Ellen's fate from me, even as we hurried downstairs and Gracie told me all the tasks I had to do. I was horribly intrigued. I was wearing the dead girl's clothing and that night would sleep in what had been her bed. I was to carry out her work in the house. It was as if she was my shadow, or I hers.

It seemed that Ellen's spirit was everywhere in the house. Gracie warned me not to mention her to the cook, Mrs Pearson, as she was the dead girl's aunt. I didn't need to, because Cook brought up the subject herself. I was set to peeling a mountain of potatoes and carrots in the kitchen. Gracie waved and ran off to clean upstairs. I stared at the vegetables and wished I was up in the main rooms too.

Mrs Pearson was as round as a cook should be. She puffed alarmingly as she walked, as if her breath caught. Her rolling gait made me hide a smile. But she was a kind woman.

'Get these spuds done and scrub them roots. I'm making chicken and meat pies and glazed carrots and mashed potatoes for dinner.'

'Sounds delicious,' I said politely.

She winked at me. 'That's for the family; but what they eat up there, we eat down here too. I'll say that for Mrs Dawton — for all her faults, she's generous with the food.'

That was a relief. The Collingtons had been too, but I'd heard stories from friends about their places where they fed on scrapings fit only for the pigs.

'Now,' she said, 'you get stuck into that lot while I make the pastry. Later, you'll change into a fresh uniform and help Gracie upstairs. There's a lot to do. My Ellen did a fine job, and I'm sure you will too.'

She stopped and sniffed. Her eyes were shiny. I glanced away, not wishing to embarrass her. She sighed. 'She was such a good girl, my niece. Such a help to me. Nothing was too much bother, and no complaints from her. She carried my bags for me on my day off, kept me company sometimes. Imagine that, a beautiful young girl like that spending time with her old auntie. That's how kind she was. She'd bring me little gifts too. She didn't deserve such a wicked end.'

It was clearly still a raw shock. I didn't know what to say, so I kept my head down and peeled the potatoes. Mrs Pearson sighed once more, then turned to the cupboards and took down the flour and bowls to make the pastry. We worked companionably for the afternoon. Once I'd done the veg, I was allowed to help prepare the stewing apples. Yet more scrubbing and peeling to be done.

When the apples were set to simmer-ing and a lovely aroma filled the kitchen, Mrs Pearson stopped our work. I was hopeful we'd eat, as I was starving. I'd missed lunch due to travelling. Mr Dawton hadn't offered to stop to eat. Bill came in to pick up a tray of afternoon tea and cakes for Mrs Dawton. I smiled, but he didn't return it. I made a face behind his back. What a grumpy sort he was.

'Right, now,' Mrs Pearson said, 'the gardeners will have to have an early meal today. I'm behind schedule. Mr Crickett has his own daily to make his meals, so you don't have to take him anything, but the two under-gardeners need theirs. It's your job to take the food over to the bothy.'

'The bothy? What's that?'

'You'll find it. Take that covered basket and go out the back door. You'll see a row of cottages; the bothy's over there.'

I wasn't going to get more help. She turned away and stirred at the large pots on the range. Her face was rosy from the heat, and a wisp of greying hair stuck out from under her cap.

I took the basket and headed out. It was nice to be outside. I found my way across the cobbled courtyard and through the stables. Then I came to the row of low cottages. Through the windows and doors I saw pots and implements and all the paraphernalia of a gardener's work. The end cottage door was open and I saw two men inside.

I went over and knocked. They turned and I lifted up the basket. 'Mrs Pearson's sent your dinner.'

One man came to get the basket. A pleasant shock rippled through me. He was handsome. Not tall, but stocky and strong-looking. He had thick, dark curling hair and blue eyes, clear like the sky. His skin was tanned from working outdoors.

'Who are you?' he asked, those beautiful eyes roaming over me.

'I'm Hannah. I arrived today.'

The other man came out too. He was older, a grizzled beard on his chin and a balding head. But he grinned in a friendly fashion. 'Hello, Hannah. What goodies have you brought us? I'm fair starving. This is Adam, and I'm Peter.'

'Pleased to meet you,' I said and dipped a small curtsey.

I could hardly take my gaze from Adam. Luckily, he didn't appear to notice. He took the basket and gave it to Peter. The older man took it quickly and rummaged in its contents. He began to lay the items out on the table in the bothy.

Adam stepped outside with me. He scratched at his hair, and I noticed the muscles flex in his forearm.

'So you're taking on Ellen's position?' he said.

I was almost sick of her name. Then I felt ashamed. The poor girl had been killed. It wasn't her fault that she was everywhere at Muirfield Hall. Of course she was still in everyone's mind. The killer had not been caught. That thought froze me for a moment. He or she was out there, somewhere.

'Yes. Did you know her well?' I found myself asking.

He shrugged. 'No better than the rest of us. She was an unhappy girl.'

'Unhappy? What do you mean?'

He didn't answer that. Instead, he gestured in the direction of the walled garden. 'Have you seen the gardens yet?'

I've only just arrived, as I told you, I thought but didn't say. Instead, I answered, 'No, I haven't seen them.'

'They are the best gardens in the region. Full of fine exotic plants you won't see anywhere else. Mr Dawton's a plant collector, you see. He's got species from America to grow that won't grow anywhere else in Scotland, or England for that matter.'

I wasn't very interested in plants or gardening. But I was interested in Adam. He was glorious to look at. I'd never seen a man so fine-looking. He exuded health and strength and . . . *maleness.* I didn't care what he said as long as I could listen. I helped the conversation along so I didn't have to leave.

'They do sound wonderful, these gardens.'

He stared at me. 'One day I'll be head gardener here. Or maybe somewhere else, somewhere bigger and better than Muirfield Hall. One of the grand estates in the south, perhaps.'

'Isn't Mr Crickett head gardener here?' I recalled Mrs Pearson's instructions. Mr Crickett was so important he had his own house and a daily maid to tend to him.

Adam's brows knitted together. They were dark, like his hair. 'He'll retire sometime. And I'll be ready to take over. I've got plans. They don't include living in this bothy with old Pete forever.' His gaze on me was assessing.

'It's good to have ambitions,' I said with a smile. I didn't have any myself — I was glad to simply have a job — but I admired him for it.

'I can show you the walled garden.'

'Yes, I'd like that,' I said, my heartbeat fast in my chest. Spending time with Adam would be no chore.

'When you get your half-day, we'll do it then.'

'I don't know when that is.'

'Well, you'll know soon enough, won't you? Come back when you're ready.'

He turned and went back into the bothy, where Pete was tucking into his dinner. I felt I'd been dismissed. Not liking that feeling, I didn't bother with goodbyes, but went back across the stables to the kitchen. Mrs Pearson wiped her forehead with her apron.

'You took your time. Don't let Mrs Smith find you dawdling. Now, change your uniform. There's dusting to be done upstairs.'

'When will we eat?' I asked.

'After the family's eaten. We eat late, in the servants' hall. Now get going, or you'll be in trouble,' she said, not unkindly.

I was curious to see the first floor of Muirfield. Here was where the life of the Dawtons was played out. As I imagined, the rooms were lovely. The decor was fine and luxurious, and the furniture and ornaments of high quality. I quite enjoyed my hours with Gracie, both of us with a feather duster, on tiptoes to reach the picture frames and the crystal glory of the wall sconces.

I let my imagination drift free as I lifted the dust from the surfaces. I thought about Mam and Dad and Kitty. It wasn't going to be easy visiting them. I wondered how long it would be before I saw their dear faces again. I comforted myself with the knowledge that at least I was not a burden to them. Goodness knew they had enough problems without having to feed and shelter me.

Then I tried to imagine what it must be like to be a lady of wealth living in such a beautiful home. That was a stretch I couldn't quite make. No, it was certainly not in my future. I had to make do with cleaning and tidying for others.

'Why did you leave your last position?' Gracie asked, stretching up to touch her feather duster to the chandelier. It made a pretty tinkling noise.

'I was asked to. Not for any scandal,' I added hurriedly when I saw her expression. 'I got ill and I didn't get well quick enough. They had to let me go.'

'That doesn't sound very fair. I've heard of people like that. They don't think nothing of what happens to their servants after they've sacked them. It's awful.' Gracie shook her head glumly.

'The Collingtons weren't like that,' I said. 'They were lovely to work for. I had to look after little Arthur, their son. He was a bright wee lad. We had many a laugh together. They paid me well and the food was good and plentiful. I even had my own room. It was painted such a shade of blue, like the sky, and had matching curtains.'

'Oh, it does sound wonderful,' Gracie sighed. 'What a pity they didn't keep you on.'

'What's it like working here?' I said, moving on from the Collingtons in case I burst out crying for what had been. 'Are you happy?'

'Happy?' Gracie said, as if she'd never considered this. 'I suppose so. I'm content, if that's what you mean. It's all right really. Mrs Smith is strict but fair, and Cook — that's Mrs Pearson — is kind even if she does shout a lot. I've got my parents in the village, so I can visit them on my day off.'

We finished with the chandelier, leaving it gleaming like diamonds. I hoped that a member of the family might come by so I could see them, but there was no sign of anyone except ourselves around. 'What now?' I asked.

Gracie scratched at her head under her cap, then set it straight over her pale brown hair. 'Now we roll up the rug and dust the floorboards. Then we get that big tin of beeswax and rub it into the chair legs until they look like chestnuts.'

I groaned. It seemed we'd never run

out of chores to do. Gracie grinned. She took one corner of the heavy embroidered rug and nodded for to me to take the other. Between us we managed to roll it back. An expanse of floorboards waited for our touch.

I felt already immersed in the life of Muirfield Hall. I hadn't met the mistress or the young ladies yet, but I was curious to see them. I liked the people I'd met today. But somewhere a murderer lurked, and I couldn't help but wonder if he or she lived on the estate. Not only that, but was it possible they would strike again?

3

Mr Joseph's Secret

I was exhausted by the time Gracie told me we were to eat. I followed her into the long servants' hall, which was dominated by a dark wood table and rows of hard-backed chairs. A scrawny girl with thin blonde hair was putting down dishes of soup. I guessed she was Janet, the scullery maid. Her apron was stained with food and her cap was awry. She had dark circles under her eyes and a hunted expression.

As we came in, she slipped, and one of the dishes crashed to the floor, sending soup and shards of ceramic flying. There was a stifled laugh and I glanced round to see a young woman, hand over mouth and eyes sly with mirth. Her maid's uniform couldn't hide her curves and glossy red hair. Her eyes were a cat's green and she had pale, lustrous skin like a lady.

'That's Sarah,' Gracie whispered, nudging me.

'What a butterfingers,' Sarah said. 'Hurry up, Janet, or Mr Joseph will see what a mess you've made.' Janet looked terrified.

'Here,' I said, going forward, 'let me help you.' I almost collided with another person who'd stepped in too. It was Bill, the footman. 'Sorry.' I smiled. 'I'm making a habit of bumping into you.'

He managed a small nod. Then he knelt and began to pick up the pieces of china. 'Go and get a wet cloth,' he told the frightened girl. 'We'll need to mop up this soup.'

'I'm starving,' Sarah said loudly behind us. 'Are we going to have to wait all night to get our food?'

I saw Bill's shoulders tense and then relax. I looked round at her and tried for a friendly tone. 'Why don't you help us clear this up? More hands make lighter work.'

She laughed; a high, brittle sound. 'No, thanks. Looks like you and Bill have it under control. I've spent all day slaving away and I'm ready to be served myself. Whenever Janet's ready. In fact, Bill, why don't you sit with me and let the new girl here clear up? I've got something I want to tell you.'

We had, in fact, picked up all the pieces by now, and both stood up. Bill hesitated and I gave him another smile of thanks and took the china from him. Sarah flicked her fingers in the direction of the empty chair beside her. Bill's mouth tightened, but I noticed as I went out towards the kitchen that he had indeed sat beside her. Her deep red curls almost touched his paler sandy hair as she leaned in and whispered to him. Anyway, it was none of my concern. I threw the broken dish into the bin. Cook was serving up the main courses onto plates.

'Come on, Hannah. Take these in for me, please.'

Janet had cleaned up the soup

splatters, and I set the laden plates down on the table. No one offered to help, and I realised it was probably my job to do this. After all, I was both kitchen and house maid. A maid of all works, it seemed.

I was about to raise my spoon and attack my soup when there was a scrape of chairs and everyone stood up. An older man, somewhat stooped but with an air of authority, had come in. 'Mr Joseph, the butler,' Gracie whispered.

'Sit, everyone, do sit please. We will say grace and then we can eat.' His voice was slow and steady and used to being obeyed, I thought.

Despite the length of the table, we were a small band. There was Mr Joseph, the butler, at the head of the table. Then to his left was Mrs Smith, the housekeeper. To his right was Mrs Pearson, the cook. Bill sat between Mrs Smith and Sarah, the lady's maid. Gracie sat next to Mrs Pearson, then there was me and finally Janet, who slid into her place as quietly as possible.

The soup was rich and excellent, made from a meat stock and generously filled with vegetables and cream. Beside me, Janet sucked at hers and nearly licked the dish clean. I was hungry too. All the new experiences of the day flashed in front of me, and I was filled with tiredness. I felt that once I'd eaten my fill, I'd like nothing more than to fall asleep. I glanced up from my musings to meet Bill's stare. For a moment we gazed at each other uncomfortably before he looked away and so did I. He had deeply brown eyes, as dark as autumn chestnuts, but not a patch on Adam's blue gaze, I thought.

Sarah frowned at me, then a smile slid onto her fine features and she enticed Bill back with another whispered conversation. Her soup lay untouched despite her earlier claim to be starving. They acted like a couple; at least she did. Perhaps they were. After all, I had no idea really about the house I now lived in and all its occupants. I decided to ask Gracie more about the people later when we went to our room.

'Sarah, if you have something to share with the assembled company, we'd be delighted to hear it,' Mr Joseph said.

She flushed, but even in her unease managed to look pretty. She shook her head. 'No, Mr Joseph. I'm just telling Bill here about the young ladies' party planned for tomorrow. They'll want the footman to let their friends in, I'm sure.'

Bill raised an eyebrow but didn't speak. He finished his soup and laid his spoon carefully down on the empty dish. What had Sarah really been saying? I didn't care. What was it to me?

A polite cough from Mr Joseph had the attention of the table. 'We have a new member of the staff arrived today. Hannah Miller is to replace Ellen.'

There was a momentary awkward silence, then he spoke again. 'We all wish you well in your new post, Hannah. Now, where is dessert?'

And that was that. I jumped up at the same time as Janet and we hurried together to get the puddings.

I was very glad to get ready for bed. After a brief wash with the pitcher of cold water, I got into my night dress and scurried under the covers. Gracie's bed creaked as she snuggled down too. We had a candle burning on the cabinet between the beds. Gracie blew it out. I smelt the smoky wick and melted wax. Such comforting smells.

I lay, staring up at the high ceiling. Moonlight bathed the room. Shadow shapes patterned the walls.

'Your first day over,' Gracie said sleepily. 'Do you think you'll like it here?'

'Yes, I'm sure I will,' I said, thinking of Adam.

'Poor Janet. She got a right mouthful from Cook for dropping that dish.' Gracie yawned.

'It was an accident. I didn't warm to Sarah; she was quite mean about it.' When there was no answer, I rolled over in bed to look at Gracie. 'Are she and Bill an item, then?'

Gracie stared back. She blinked and shook her head. 'Not anymore, but Sarah would like to be again. It's obvious.'

'So they did step out before?'

'It was a few months ago. Bill was smitten with her and he'd been asking her out for ages. All of a sudden, she said yes. So he was courting her. And then . . . '

'What?' I said, impatiently.

'Well, I suppose it's no secret,' Gracie said, sitting up as if feeling more awake. 'It turned out she was also stepping out with a footman up at the Manor. You won't know it as you're not from around here, but there's a big estate some miles away, further up the glen. It's bigger than Muirfield and there's more money. They're gentry. The staff there think they're above us. Maybe they are. After all, everyone knows Mr Joseph's got his heart set on being butler there. He's just waiting for the old butler to die or hang up his boots. Then he's going to apply. Very taken with his lordship, is Mr Joseph. Mrs Joseph, too. Keeps pushing him to apply now. Wouldn't do any good, would it? No one needs two butlers, do they? Even if they're very rich.'

I wasn't interested in Mr Joseph's ambitions. I wanted to hear about Bill. 'How did Bill find out about the other footman?'

Gracie rubbed her nose. 'It was Ellen who told him.'

'She did the right thing.'

'Did she?'

'Of course. The truth's always best.'

'Only, it's made Bill so sad ever since. So, I wonder . . . ' Gracie frowned. 'I wonder if it was right.'

'Maybe Ellen couldn't keep the secret. Imagine the guilt of knowing but not saying.'

Gracie looked uncomfortable. 'See,

thing is, Ellen was my friend, like I told you. But . . . well, she was a funny sort of girl.'

'What do you mean?'

'She liked to know stuff about people. She got a kick out of it. Sometimes she was in such a gloom, a darkness over her, and then the next day she'd be bright as a button. She was such a moody sort. You had to tread carefully with her. She'd jump down your throat at the tiniest thing, or she'd bring you a gift. It could be unsettling. I never was sure where I was with her.'

'So she told Bill to make trouble? To split him and Sarah up?'

Gracie nodded. 'That's what I think. Somehow she found out about the footman up at the Manor. And it was too good to keep to herself. She hated Sarah.'

There, I didn't blame her. I hadn't liked what I'd seen of the lady's maid so far.

'But it was Bill who suffered. Sarah's

very confident. But Bill, he's very tender-hearted. I'm sure he was in love with Sarah.'

'They were friendly enough tonight at dinner.'

'Sarah's sure she can get him back. It's just a matter of time.' Gracie let out a huge yawn.

'Will Bill take her back?' I was a bit disappointed in him, if that was the case. Men were so easily taken in by a pretty face.

There was no answer.

'Gracie?' I hissed.

There was a loud snore. I sighed and turned back so that I could watch the moonlight.

* * *

The days went swiftly by, and soon I'd been there a fortnight. I learned all the tasks I had to do. It was hard work, but I liked being some hours in the kitchen and some upstairs. I found plenty to look at. Besides, I had Gracie for company, at least upstairs. She was becoming a good friend. Downstairs, Mrs Pearson was too old to be a friend, but was kind to me. Janet was too young and anxious. So at those periods, I was left to my own thoughts a lot. Bill was in and out of the kitchen to fetch trays of drinks and pretty snacks. I wanted to talk to him, but he ignored me. Upstairs, Sarah ignored me too whenever she had to pass me in the corridor. But with her, it was with an uplifted nose as if she smelt something bad.

A few days after I started, I met Mrs Dawton. I was feather dusting the painting frames in the long corridor on the second floor. I had to stand on tiptoe to try to reach them. Some were so high up, I knew I'd have to fetch a chair to dust them.

I was considering which chair would be allowed, when a door was flung open. Mrs Dawton appeared in a rustle of silk crinoline. She was wearing a gorgeous dark pink dress with a rose-coloured tasselled shawl over her shoulders. I remembered to curtsey. Instead of a friendly nod, she told me coldly to bring Mrs Smith to her. Her dainty cap quivered with annoyance.

I hurried to find Mrs Smith. She came back upstairs with me, worried in case it was about the day's menu. She'd already told Mrs Pearson what needed cooking. If Mrs Dawton wanted it all changed, it was going to be a lot of work. She needn't have worried. It wasn't about the menu. It was about me.

As I stood there, invisible, Mrs Dawton asked Mrs Smith to remind me that when members of the family were met with, I was to turn my face to the wall and remain entirely still and silent until the person had gone. I felt my face turning red. I had to stand there like an idiot while Mrs Smith repeated what her employer had just said. Then Mrs Smith asked me to carry on with the dusting. Mrs Dawton swept away on her wide skirts, looking outraged.

If Mrs Dawton was horrible, then her daughter Emily was quite the opposite. I was scrubbing dirt from carrots one morning when she floated into the kitchen. She was a dainty creature with tiny wrists, high cheekbones and a halo of yellow hair. Mrs Pearson greeted her warmly.

'Hello, Miss Emily. How are we today?'

'Who's that, Cook?' Emily asked, pointing at me.

I was taken aback by her bluntness, but there was nothing but curiosity in her round blue eyes.

'That, Miss Emily, is our new maid, Hannah,' Mrs Pearson said with a wink at me.

'Hannah.' She considered that, her head tilted. 'I like that name.'

'Well, that's nice,' Mrs Pearson laughed. 'I'll let Hannah bring you a biscuit while I go and see Mrs Smith about all the lovely things you'll be dining on tonight.'

She left me alone with Miss Emily. I took the lid off the biscuit tin and offered her one of the cook's fine baking treats. She took her time, slowly gazing at its contents before taking a ginger biscuit. Then she nibbled on it, seemingly savouring each tiny bite. She stared at me as I went about my work. After a short while, it felt like an itch between my shoulder blades, her watching me silently. What an odd child. For child she was, despite being twelve. At twelve, girls like me were already in service or working on a farm or elsewhere. But for the rich there was more time. I had the feeling that whether rich or poor, Miss Emily would be a child, young for her years, wherever she was.

'I have dreams,' she said suddenly.

'Do you, miss?' I wasn't sure how to react.

'Yes, Hannah, I do,' she replied solemnly. 'I see things.'

'That's nice,' I said lamely.

She shook her head vigorously at that. 'Oh, no, it's not nice. Not nice at all, mostly.'

'Are they nightmares, then?'

'They are shadows and empty gardens. There's people too, very big people.'

That made no sense at all. I put the last of the carrots to one side. 'Would you like another biscuit, miss?'

'Yes, please. Cook makes the best biscuits.'

She worked her way through another ginger round quietly while I cleaned up the sink. She was easy enough company. Whether or not she should be in the kitchen wasn't for me to decide. I wondered what Mrs Dawton would make of it, though. Her younger daughter, chatting with the kitchen maid.

'Thank you for the food, Hannah,' she said politely, hopping up from the stool she'd sat on. 'I have to go now.'

'Goodbye, miss.'

'I'll be back to see you,' she said with a frown, 'so, it's not really goodbye.'

When she'd gone, I shook my head at her strangeness. Mrs Pearson appeared back with her list and a frown. She glanced around. 'Miss Emily gone, then?'

'Yes; she ate a couple of your ginger biscuits, then told me about her dreams and that she'd be back to visit again.'

'Ah, her dreams.' Mrs Pearson nodded sagely. 'Poor wee soul.'

'What's wrong?'

'She doesn't just dream, you see. She sleepwalks. She's been found in various places in the house. If the door's open, she can get into the grounds too. No one knows why she does it. Mr Dawton had the doctor in. He gave her a draught that made her sleep very soundly, but then it made her sick. So they stopped that.'

'Couldn't they lock her door at night?'

'They tried, but she got very agitated; hysterical in fact. So now we've all got orders to look out for her, and if we see her, to take her back to her room.'

'I'll remember to do that.' It was possible, I supposed, that she might appear in the attic room and give myself and Gracie a shock. Just as well to know what was going on.

'I should've told you sooner,' Mrs Pearson said as if reading my mind. 'It didn't occur to me because she's been fine the last while.'

I was sent by Mrs Pearson a while later to ask Mr Joseph for a bottle of poor wine to steep the beef in. I knew that the butler kept the wines and spirits in a special locked cupboard and wrote what was used in a ledger. He raised an eyebrow at the sight of me.

'Cook sent me for a bottle of wine,' I said. 'She's making a meat stew,' I added hastily, in case he thought Mrs Pearson wanted to drink the stuff instead.

'Come in.'

I went into the butler's domain. He took a key and unlocked a large cupboard. His body blocked most of my view, but as I moved aside, I caught a glimpse of the contents. He looked over his shoulder, and a flash of anger and something else rippled over his features. At that moment I had no idea what I'd done to deserve this.

Later, much later, lying in my attic bed and staring at the ceiling as usual, I played it over in my head. Gracie snored gently in the bed beside me. What had the cupboard looked like? Why had Mr Joseph been so angry? I tried to see the inside of the cupboard once more. There had been endless rows of bottles — dark green, almost purple-black, and clear glass too, filled with wine and beer and spirits. There had been a gap on the middle shelf. It had struck me as out of place. As if some bottles had been put aside.

Was that it? Was Mr Joseph siphoning off wines for himself? Or to sell on to others? I stopped right there. I had no right to think such a thing of a respectable man. He was the butler, after all. The highest of the high in the servants' ranks. While I was almost the lowest, only poor Janet below me.

Maybe I was wrong. But what if I was right? And what if Ellen had somehow found out Mr Joseph's secret? If he was found to be stealing from the household, he'd lose all chance of promotion, of moving on to the big house that Gracie had mentioned. What would he do to keep Ellen silent?

A sudden shiver made me hug the bedclothes to me.

4

The Walled Garden

Without a conscious decision, I began to think about tracking down Ellen's killer. It was as if the house was holding its breath, waiting for an answer. I slept in the dead girl's bed, I had inherited her clothes, I heard stories about her from Gracie and Mrs Pearson and others. Good stories and bad. She'd been a complicated person, by all accounts. So complicated that someone had taken her life. But why? It niggled at me daily.

What had she done to anger her murderer? Or had she simply been in the wrong place at the wrong time? If that was so, what had she witnessed that meant she had to be silenced forever? It made my head ache. And yet, who was I to think I could solve a murder where a detective, brought all the way from London, could not? Perhaps I had a chance he had not. I was embedded into the household at Muirfield, whereas he was an outsider, an observer. I had a real chance to get to know everyone and their hidden depths. Of course, if Ellen had been killed by an outsider, that meant nothing.

So my musings rambled on while I worked each day. The village policeman often came to visit, making himself known and asking questions. His presence was no doubt intended to warn the killer that the law had not given up on Ellen's case. However, nothing came of it.

I was more interested in a snippet of conversation I heard between Mrs Pearson and Mr Joseph. I wasn't eavesdropping but I couldn't help but hear their conversation. I was in the servants' dining hall, cleaning the chairs and ready to wax proper the long table. Janet was in the kitchen. Everyone else was upstairs tending to the demands of Mrs Dawton, while Mr Dawton was on a visit to Glasgow.

'But where does she go?' I heard Mrs Pearson say.

'I have no idea, and it is none of our business what Mrs Smith does on her day off,' Mr Joseph replied, sounding reproving. Their voices came from the corridor outside.

'But you must admit it's strange,' Cook persisted. 'I mean, it's the same every afternoon she has off. She puts on her black coat and hat and stays out until late.'

'She must be visiting with family.' Mr Joseph now sounded as if he was losing his patience with the conversation.

'But she doesn't have any family. She told me that years ago. There's just her since Mr Smith died. No children and no siblings.'

'There's no great mystery, Mrs Pearson,' Mr Joseph said. 'Why are you making it one? She must be visiting a friend. Come along, there's much to do today. I can't stand here making idle gossip.'

I heard the click of his shoes and

then a murmured 'Well, goodness me' from Cook. I hunkered down and made a big deal of cleaning the chair struts. They needed it. If Mrs Pearson popped her head round, she'd see me hard at work. In any event, she didn't, and I was left wondering where Mrs Smith vanished to on her days off.

Before long, that wondering turned to a resolve to find out. I was due my first half-day off that week and was looking forward to it. It was too far to go home, and I had planned a short walk in the country and then a good read of my book. But now I decided I'd use it to follow the housekeeper.

So it was with great anticipation that I finished up my duties that lunch-time and then put on my outdoor coat and hat. I was pleased with my outfit. The dark green colours went well with my brown hair and I had finally got rid of the last weaknesses left by the influenza. My colour was high and I felt strong, full of energy despite the hard work that Muirfield demanded. I decided that while I would never be pretty, I looked attractive enough. Clear skin and youth were to my advantage.

I had planned to go outside into the side garden and linger there until I spied Mrs Smith leaving the house. Then, somehow, I'd follow her without the housekeeper being aware. I had no clear idea how I'd achieve that, but felt confident I'd manage somehow.

I was almost enjoying myself. I had to remind myself that this was my detective work and that sobered me up quickly. Whatever I did to discover Ellen's murderer might very well put me in the path of a dangerous person too.

The trouble was, it was too nice a day to think such dark thoughts. I found myself humming a tune as I skipped downstairs and out the side door. The gardens here, on the opposite side from the walled gardens, were plain grass lawns and shrubberies. In this season, as autumn took its grip, there was little colour to be seen. The shrubs were green- or brown-leaved and the grass dull. The air, however, was light and cool, and I took great breaths of it, glad to be outside.

A small cough made me spin round, my heart beating faster. I was edgy, and hadn't realised just how much so. The person standing there was a surprise. The last person I'd expected. It was Bill.

'It's your day off,' he said. Not a question but rather a statement.

I nodded. 'Finally, it is. I've been here weeks, stuck in the house.'

'Apart from your daily trip to the bothy with the gardeners' lunches.'

'I don't think that a ten-minute round walk is enough each day,' I said tartly.

He flushed slightly. I was a little annoyed with him. How dare he comment on my visits to Adam? Not that I'd seen much of him. Usually it was old Pete who was there to take the basket of food. Mostly, no one was around and I'd leave the basket in the bothy, disappointed yet again not to see Adam. Piqued too, if truth be told, that he didn't appear to be seeking me out. I had not interested him in the way he had interested me.

'It's my day off too,' Bill said.

'That's nice. Does Sarah get the same hours off?' I assumed he and Sarah would spend their free time together.

His eyebrows fused for a moment in confusion. 'No, she doesn't. Why does that . . . Anyway, I wanted to ask you . . . '

At that precise moment, I glimpsed the short figure of Mrs Smith hurrying down the long driveway. As Cook had described, she was wearing a black coat and wide black hat, and in one hand she carried a long, thin umbrella, also black. She was prepared for all weathers.

I had to hurry before I lost sight of her. Bill was standing there, trying to say something. I didn't have time to listen.

'I'm sorry, I have to go.'

'But I haven't asked you yet — would you like to go into the village with me? There's a very nice tea room there.'

'I really have to go,' I said desperately, seeing Mrs Smith reach the bend in the trees.

I left him there and walked fast, almost at a trot, to catch up with the housekeeper. All my focus was on her. Bill was forgotten, and even Adam was pushed to the back of my mind. I sped up to the bend and then slowed as I turned it. There she was. She was making good speed for a small woman. I waited until she reached the gatehouse and turned left. Then I hurried forward. I wasn't worried. I knew I could walk for miles now I was returned to good health.

It never occurred to me that she might have arranged transport to get away from Muirfield. I had assumed she'd walk over the fields to wherever she was going. The village wasn't far away, about a half hour's walk through country lanes. But when I reached the gatehouse and turned left, I saw Mrs Smith climbing up into a wagon. I flattened myself against the stone wall as the wagon passed, the horses clip-clopping merrily as the driver flicked the reins. She didn't notice me, too busy arranging her skirts and then sitting up with a straight back as she was whisked away.

In a gloomy mood, I walked slowly back up the drive. My adventure was over for the day, and my previous notion to have a walk and read my book didn't appeal anymore. Bill had gone from the garden. I didn't blame him. I'd been rather rude in my rush to follow Mrs Smith. He probably would never speak to me again.

Then I remembered Adam's promise. *I can show you the walled garden.* On my half-day, he'd said; we'd do it then. Was it me, or did the day suddenly brighten? My steps took me round the back of the house to the bothy and the greenhouses. Where was Adam?

I found him in the second greenhouse. He didn't see me at first and I was able to drink in the sight of him.

He was pruning plants in pots on a shelf. His thick dark hair looked carelessly mussed, and his shoulders were broad as he went about his work. He wore a leather jerkin and breeches that showed off the powerful muscles in his legs. There was a butterfly flutter in my stomach as I approached.

'Hello,' I said, leaning in at the greenhouse door.

He flicked me a glance, looked away for a minute at his plants and then back at me. He grinned and lowered his hands from his task. I noticed they were brown with soil, the fingernails blackened. They were working hands.

'Hannah Miller. Your day off then?' He nodded at my coat.

I touched at the rim of my hat and nodded. I hoped he liked the look of me. He wiped a dirty hand across his forehead, leaving a soil smear. Strangely, it added to his good looks. There was a smell of male sweat and it prickled at my nose, not unpleasantly.

'Yes, my day off. You said you'd show

me Mr Dawton's walled garden,' I said boldly.

He eyed me. To be the attention of his intense blue gaze was glorious. 'So I did, so I did,' he said slowly.

'Shall we?' I moved back from the greenhouse onto the slabbed ground.

It was oddly like enticing a large cat to play; a fleeting fancy that made me smile inside. Yet, weren't large cats dangerous when provoked? Adam was perfectly polite as he followed me out and indicated the way to the walled garden. In fact, he seemed eager to educate me about it.

'It's Mr Dawton's pride and joy,' he said as we reached the green-painted door inserted into the thick stone walls. 'Wait until you see the plants we've got growing in here.'

I knew I wouldn't understand a thing about them. One plant looked pretty much like another to me. In fact, I'd never really considered plants. They existed but they never entered my thoughts. The opposite was true of Adam. He was a fount of knowledge about them. And he shared it with me. As I listened to him, I decided that wasn't entirely true. He wasn't waiting to see if I understood or even if I was interested. It was as if I was a soft surface off which to bounce his voice. I stifled a yawn.

I had to admit that inside the walls, the garden was rather lovely. Here, unlike the side garden, there were blooms still on show. A rainbow of glory. A few petals were dropping here and there, but most were intact. Even I could see that there was a variety of different leaf shapes and shades. There was an odd-looking tree with flowers like bottle brushes. Another had great leaves with slashed gaps in them. These were unlike anything I'd ever seen before.

'It's very sheltered here, that's why it prolongs the growing season,' Adam said.

I nodded. Despite my ignorance, I found myself intrigued by the strange things.

'Look at this,' Adam said, taking my arm to guide me to a small tree.

I felt a thrill of electricity travel up my limbs. His touch, warm and firm, felt impressed on my very skin through the wool of my coat. He took his hand away and it was as if I'd suffered a loss.

'There,' he pointed.

It was, as I say, a small tree but peculiar. I can't rightly describe it, but it was jagged like a bundle of snakes on a stick.

'This is a very rare tree,' Adam said. 'The jewel of Mr Dawton's collection. They call it a monkey puzzle.'

'Why is it called that?' I asked, for want of something to say. He clearly expected me to be impressed with the tree.

'I suppose because it would puzzle a monkey to climb it,' he said. 'It's very prickly.'

'Of course.' I fell silent, unsure where to take the conversation and unwilling to let Adam go. Inspiration struck. 'So, Mr Dawton . . . he's very taken with plants, is he?'

He looked at me as if I was a fool. I

blushed and pretended to peer at the monkey puzzle to hide my hot face. He'd already told me Mr Dawton was passionate about his gardens. If only I could get Adam talking about some other topics. For example, what kind of food did he like? Did he enjoy walking in the countryside? Was he courting? I wouldn't have minded going to the village tea room with Adam.

'I told you, he's a plant collector. These are the best gardens around for miles. All these plants . . . ' He spread his arms. ' . . . they're exotics you'll likely never see anywhere else.'

'Goodness,' I said, sounding silly. But really, what else was there to say?

His lip curled sullenly and he looked all of a sudden younger. 'Why did I think you could understand? You're naught but a girl. You've never stepped outside the county. This is way above your head.'

I wanted to shout at him that actually I came from a county over, so he was wrong there! But I knew what he meant. I was an ignorant girl who knew nothing of the world. He was right. But I didn't want to lose his interest. What small interest he had in me, that was.

He'd turned to the door. 'Adam!' I called desperately.

He turned around slowly, that curled lip still in place. His dark good looks twisted my gut somewhere deep down.

'Adam,' I called more softly. 'Teach me, then. You're right, I don't know much, but I'd like to. You know so much, so tell me.'

In an instant his expression changed. Gone was the surly disappointment in me. In its stead, a grin slowly spread across his face with an assurance of his worth. I'd soothed his ego. I'd told him he was better than me. I'd humbled myself. It left a slight sour taste in my mouth, but anything was better than losing him.

'You see, it's my cultivation of these plants that's brought them to life. I've taken care of the seedlings that get sent here and experimented with how to care for them. It's thanks to me that Mr Dawton has such a fine collection.'

'What about Peter? Does he cultivate them too?'

'Aye, he does.' His voice was flat.

I realised it was the wrong thing to say. 'But I'll guess you're better at it than him.'

'Peter's old so he's got old ways. I've got a gift for it. Mr Dawton's always telling me that.'

'So how does Mr Dawton get his seeds?' I warmed to my theme.

This wasn't so difficult. Keeping Adam's attention needed only a prompt or two, and he was quite willing to take the floor while I was quite willing to be the eager listener. That way I could concentrate on the way his hair curled around the lobes of his ears; and the length of his dark lashes, almost feminine, against his tanned skin. How could a man's eyes be so sharply and perfectly blue? Why did he smell of sweat and leather and earth in a heady mixture that made me want to inhale forever?

'He writes to other plant collectors. They exchange seeds and compete to grow them. And of course he buys from America. He's got contacts there. It's big business.'

'What do you do on your day off?' I asked.

He looked surprised. Then he shrugged. 'Not much. I tend the plants.'

I perked up at that. Adam had no girl he was courting. That was good news.

'There's a good tea room in the village, I've heard,' I said. 'Perhaps we could go there.'

'I'm working.'

'Oh, I didn't mean now.' Except that was what I had meant. I'd forgotten he wasn't free. I was too keen.

'Anyway, I don't go much to the village. I've got everything I need right here.'

'You must leave sometimes. What about your family? Don't you visit them?'

'I don't have family.' He was abrupt.

There was a silence between us. I'd run out of things to say. I was bored by

Adam's plants. And he apparently was bored by me. I could tell by his vacant expression. He was thinking about something. But it wasn't me.

'I've got to go,' he said finally.

I didn't try to stop him. The truth was, I couldn't think of a way to make him stay. I watched him leave through the door in the wall. Then I went out too. I went back to the house, thinking that I'd read my book after all.

Gracie grabbed me excitedly. 'I've been looking for you. Guess what?'

'What?'

'A bit more enthusiasm, Hannah, please. I've just heard from Cook that there's going to be a house party.'

'What's that to the likes of me and you?' I was harsh with disappointment over Adam.

She ignored my bad mood. 'You've never experienced one at Muirfield. Mr Dawton invites his Glasgow friends to come for the game shooting. The wives are entertained by Mrs Dawton. There's dancing and cards and huge dinners.

But, best of all, the servants get a party too with such lovely food and drink. And . . . ' She was almost curling up with happiness.

'And?' I smiled. It was hard to stay grumpy when Gracie was the opposite.

'And . . . ' She plucked at my sleeve. ' . . . there's a young man I like. He's a footman with the Howie family and usually he comes with them. Oh, Hannah, I can't wait.'

'It does sound nice.'

'That's putting it mildly.' Then she frowned. 'By the way, any idea what's wrong with Bill? He's in a terrible bad mood.'

I felt a flash of shame. 'No,' I lied, 'I don't know.'

I slunk upstairs, hoping not to see the footman. I was fairly certain I was the cause of his anger. Well, I thought, settling down on my bed with my book, I didn't owe him anything. He'd find someone else to go to the tea room with. Sarah must get days off too. A little worm of guilt remained, but I ignored it as I delved into my penny dreadful.

I read the rest of the afternoon and on into the evening after dinner. I finished with quite a sore head from squinting in the candlelight until the heroine got her happy-ever-after. With a sigh of contentment, I closed the book. From downstairs, there came the sound of a door opening and closing. Most probably it was Mrs Smith returning from her mysterious outing. I resolved, there and then, to follow her again and find out where she went to.

5

The Summerhouse

Before any start could be made on preparing for the house party, Gracie was called home. Mrs Smith told her that a message had come to say her mother was ill.

'You're to go immediately.'

'It must be bad then,' Gracie said, dismayed.

The housekeeper shook her head. 'I don't know; that's just what the message was from the boy at the kitchen door. She's to come at once, he said. Luckily the family are all out of the house, so we won't be as busy today. In fact, Hannah can go with you.'

Gracie glanced gratefully at me. Her eyes were shiny with unshed tears, and my heart went out to her. If anything happened to my own mother, I'd be devastated. Poor Gracie. I prayed that whatever it was, Gracie's mother would recover.

'Come, we'll fetch our coats,' I said, putting my arm round her shoulders.

'I need you back here before dinner,' Mrs Smith said. 'The family might be out, but we are all here, and Cook will need help to prepare the food. And I can't have Mrs Dawton complaining tomorrow about the lack of dusting, can I?'

Her voice was strict but her face was kind, and she touched Gracie's arm in sympathy. I thought how lucky we were to have a housekeeper who cared for those under her rule. It could be quite different. All in all, I'd landed on my feet coming to Muirfield Hall, and I wanted to keep my position. There were many terrible places hiring servants and treating them no better than slaves.

We put on our coats and hats and walked down into the village. The day was overcast and gloomy, matching Gracie's mood. A threat of rain hung over us in the black clouds. The damp grasses fanned our skirts, leaving seeds on the material that we brushed away. The wood pigeons cooed sorrowfully in the branches. At one point, a fox leapt across the lane in front of us, making us both jump.

'What'll I do without my mum?' Gracie said then.

'You don't yet know what ails her,' I comforted her as best I could. 'It may be nothing.'

'Can't be nothing if I'm told to hoof it right away,' came the glum reply.

I hooked my arm in hers, and we walked as quickly as possible on the bumpy ground down into the huddle of village houses. The village wasn't much more than a crowd of dwellings surrounded by hedgerows and fields. Harvesting was going on, and there was a flurry of activity as hay bales rose up, then the glint and slice of the scythes and the shouts of the men. I followed Gracie down a muddy path to a small house. It was old and hunched, as if the bricks were collapsing in on each other. The slates were like grey teeth, overlapping in an overfull mouth. She pushed open the grimy door.

I hesitated, not sure if I was to go in. Gracie beckoned me.

'Come along, Hannah. Come and meet my brothers and sisters.'

Inside was small and dark and full of bodies. I counted five small children. The smallest was a baby crawling on the hearth while the rest were set to tasks. One girl was sewing while another stoked up the fire. A young boy cleaned boots and another was layering peat sods by the fireside. They looked up curiously at us but didn't stop what they were doing. Gracie went and kissed each of them fondly. My eyes adjusted, and then I saw a woman bustling forward, arms outstretched.

'Gracie, my darling, here you are.'

'Mum! What's wrong with you? Are you going to be all right?'

'Sure I am, my darling, sure I am.' She gathered Gracie in a great hug that set her cotton mob cap quivering. 'And who's this with you?'

'I'm Hannah Miller,' I said politely with a dip of a curtsey. 'I work with Gracie up at Muirfield. We were sent on account of your illness.' I tried to keep reproof from my voice, as it seemed to me there was nothing ailing Gracie's mother at all. What was going on?

'Ah, yes. Don't fret, Gracie dear. I'm as hale and hearty as always. Sit yourselves down.'

She wouldn't say more until she'd cleared a few children, who'd clambered up to listen, from the ancient settle by the fire and made us sit there. She sat on a kitchen stool and smoothed out her apron before explaining. A child brought tea and I sipped it, hot and strongly brewed.

'I said I was ill because it was the only way I could get you to come home quickly. I had to speak to you,' she said. 'I want you to pack up at Muirfield, hand in your notice today.'

Gracie stared at her mother, open-mouthed in astonishment. 'Why would I do that?'

'Because you're in danger there. It's that murder, see. That Ellen Munroe getting herself killed. It's not right. And it's not safe.'

Gracie shook her head. 'But why now? Ellen's murder was terrible, but it was weeks ago. Why are you suddenly wanting me home now?'

'Because he's killed again,' Gracie's mother said.

The dramatic echo of her voice rang in my ears. 'Who's the victim?' I asked, when Gracie said nothing.

She looked at me, then back at her daughter. 'It's Alice Litton's girl, May. She's vanished.'

'Vanished? So there's no body?' Gracie had found her voice. 'How do you know she was murdered?'

'Stands to reason, doesn't it?' her mother said darkly. 'Girls don't go missing just like that. There's foul play involved. Why else would she up and go with no word to anyone and all her belongings left in the cottage?'

Gracie rolled her eyes. 'If it's May

Litton, then there's all sorts of explanations as to why she'd disappear.' She turned to me. 'I doubt she's been murdered. May's very popular with the local boys. It's a lot more likely she's gone off with her latest suitor.'

'And what would the motive be for killing her?' I asked, more to myself than to the others.

'Someone out there who's pure evil. Don't need a motive other than that,' Gracie's mother said simply.

She had a point. But so did Gracie. It sounded as if this May Litton had decided to leave the village. If her suitor didn't suit her family, then they might just flit away without telling a soul.

'I don't like it. I want you to come home.' Gracie's mother was firm.

'I can't,' Gracie cried. 'Firstly, we need the money I bring in; and secondly, I like working there. Especially now that Hannah's with me.'

'You'll do what you're told!'

'And if I don't?'

'Well . . . '

'How about this,' I interrupted as politely as possible before the two women started a fight. 'What if Gracie could keep working at the Hall but we both were very careful and kept a look out for anything suspicious? We could be wary of everyone and never let ourselves be alone with one other person at any time. It does seem a shame for Gracie to give up her job. I'm sure her wages must be very welcome.'

I hit a nerve mentioning Gracie's wages, I was sure. Gracie's family were not well off. There was a large passel of mouths to feed. The little house was ramshackle. I assumed Gracie's father was one of the men harvesting in the fields. The work was seasonal and the income low. Maybe Gracie had the only regular source of money coming into the household. Her mother's fear had to be great, to consider taking that away.

'Mmm, I don't know . . . '

'Oh please, Mum. That's a sensible idea from Hannah — you know it is,'

Gracie wheedled.

'All right. For now you can keep working there,' her mother decided. 'But should I think different, I'll send for you.'

She offered more tea and a doorstop of bread, but Gracie refused.

'Mrs Smith's been kind to let me come here, and I don't want to take advantage of it. How will I tell her you're not ill after all?'

'A wee white lie won't harm her.'

'Oh Mum, you're terrible.' Gracie kissed her cheek and gave her a hug.

We parted on good terms, and all the children came out of the house to wave goodbye to their sister.

'Honestly, she could've waited until my day off to tell me that,' Gracie puffed as we walked back up the slope towards Muirfield.

'I suppose May Litton's vanishing act alarmed her so.'

'Mum's very impulsive. I pray she won't change her mind again and force me to leave the Dawtons.'

'We must make sure she doesn't.'

I pulled at a grass stem while I thought about this, working it into a lover's knot. A light drizzle of rain floated on the breeze. It moistened our coats, and I smelt the damp wool and a waft of lavender and mothballs. The ribbons on my hat hung down until I pushed them back. A stitch was needed. My wages had not yet materialised, and I made a mental note to ask Mrs Smith when I might receive them.

'And how do we do that?' Gracie asked.

'Do what?' I'd been lost in thinking what I'd spend my money on, apart from ribbons and wages sent home to my parents.

'You said we'd make sure Mum doesn't send for me,' Gracie said impatiently.

'Sorry, yes I did. I suppose we do it by being careful.' I didn't want to tell Gracie that I was already playing detective. Besides, what had I done except try to find out what Ellen had been like? I had to try harder. I needed to find a motive. Why had someone taken Ellen's life? If I could find out, then Gracie could keep her job. Suddenly it mattered a great deal. It was no longer a kind of a game, a mystery and a curiosity for idle hours. Gracie had become a good friend. I'd miss her terribly if she left the Hall.

'I can't be more careful. Besides, when do I get the chance to be alone with someone? Not ever, not likely. I'm so bloomin' busy scrubbing on my knees or dusting the ceilings,' she grumbled.

'What about at the house party? When your young man comes calling,' I teased.

She blushed beetroot red. 'I can't say I'll be alone with Johnny either. That wouldn't be right.'

'Let life go on as it will,' I suggested. 'But you can go home next week on your afternoon off and reassure your mother that all is well. If she sees you calm and happy each week, she'll soon forget to worry about you.'

Gracie looked less than convinced but nodded. Then she looked serious. 'I don't agree with Mum about there being a man out there killing young women. I think Ellen knew something that got her killed. She was that kind of girl.'

'I think you're right. But what was it?'

'Could be all sorts of things. I told you, she liked knowing stuff about people. Look at the way she found out about Sarah and that footman. I'll bet there were others who could be hurt by what she knew. Someone's secret was so powerful that they had to stop her.'

And I thought with surprise how clever my friend was. How shrewdly she'd pinpointed my very own thoughts about Ellen Munroe.

Later that afternoon, I was sent with a late basket of food to the bothy. Mrs Pearson was at sixes and sevens, having decided to clear out the cupboards in advance of the house party. I left her surrounded by a heap of bowls and plates. Janet was running around like a cat on hot tiles. Every so often, the cook would bellow an instruction for her. I knew I wouldn't be missed for a while. I'd made up my mind to slip away and visit the summerhouse and lake where Ellen had met her end.

I hoped to see Adam, but he wasn't at the bothy. I went inside and set the basket on the battered wooden table. I looked about for a sign he'd been around. It was a neat place. I knew that was Peter's doing. I'd seen the older man sweeping the floor. Whenever he was there to take the basket, he made a good show of cleaning the table before laying out the food.

I was touched to see a small glass jar with a posy of late flowers in it. I leaned in to smell them. There was a faint scent of lilac. Had Adam set it there? It was hard to imagine him doing so. The act needed tenderness. Did I then think that Adam was incapable of being tender? I didn't know. Yet I hoped he could be. I found him so attractive. I wanted fervently for him to find me so too. Then, if we were courting, I'd like him to be gentle and kind and, yes, *tender* to me. With confused emotions, I straightened the cloth over the basket and went outside.

I glanced back towards the house. There was no one visible. The windows were blanks, reflecting white light back at me. No sign of Mrs Smith or of Cook or Mr Joseph. Mrs Pearson was most likely burrowing into the back of the endless kitchen cupboards. Mrs Smith I had seen earlier organising the day girls who came in to use the copper for the Dawtons' laundry. That was likely to take all day.

As for Mr Joseph, I hadn't noticed his whereabouts. But he rarely ventured outside. His domain was the innards of Muirfield Hall. And with Gracie, Janet and Bill, even if they saw me, they wouldn't tell. Sarah was another matter. If she had been watching from an upstairs window I'd be in big trouble.

Luckily, she was with Mrs Dawton out visiting in the city.

With anticipation, I headed in the direction away from the house. I'd not been further than the bothy and its attached cottages before. After the cottages and the row of long greenhouses, to either side the woodlands began. Great oak trees and silvery birches dominated. Here and there the deep red berries clustered on rowans. A few thrushes flew up from feeding on them.

The woodlands fringed the estate. I felt it was possible to get lost in them. However, the summerhouse and the large lake were in a wide clearing and in a direct line from the bothy. I'd be safe enough finding my way back.

It was raining now, the drizzle earlier having thickened into proper droplets. I wished I'd brought a cloak or umbrella. As I reached the summerhouse, it looked a bleak sort of place. Out of season and in the wrong weather. It was meant for searing-hot sunny days with boating on the lake and picnics and champagne. Now its painted wooden walls were trickled with rain and the door facing the lake was firmly shut.

I stepped up onto a wooden raised platform on which the summerhouse was built. For a moment I stared out at the lake. Its surface was grey and pitted with the rain. The edge was fringed with slimy water plants. I shivered, thinking of Ellen and where her body had ended up. It wasn't a pleasant thought. The margins of the lake were muddy. I remembered Gracie's words. *There were signs of a scuffle in the mud at the edge of the lake.* Someone had followed Ellen here and pushed her in until she drowned.

There was a boat floating on the lake, tied to a stake. Further out, a flotilla of ducks rose and dived with an occasional squawking cry. At the far shore, the woodlands began in earnest. They were a dark blanket to my horizon. In fact, the trees were all around me. If I glanced back, I'd see only trunks and low branches, maybe the scuttling of a squirrel. Of course, I'd see the path too, I thought comfortingly.

I was suddenly and utterly aware of the isolation. It was as if the summerhouse was miles from anywhere, instead of a short walk from the house. I realised it had been designed that way. It provided a quiet retreat, or a perfect summer party venue, depending on one's mood. I was quite alone.

Determined not to be scared, I walked on the platform round to the summerhouse door. I pulled at the door knob. For a second it didn't budge, and I thought it must be locked. But then, with more force, the door sprang open. An aroma of cured wood, mould and something unidentified hit my nose.

I stepped inside. The door swung shut on creaking hinges behind me. There was a large space within, a circular room with a wooden shelf all around at the height for sitting on. The shelf was covered in large, long cushions. I sat for a moment. The cushions were faintly damp. Still, I imagined being a visitor to the Dawtons in the summer. I imagined the good food packed by Mrs Pearson into a picnic hamper to be brought here. The young men pouring wine for the ladies. The laughter and good cheer. The inevitable boat trip across the lake, to be followed perhaps by a walk in the woods. Then I sighed. It was a life far different from mine. It was only ever possible in a dream.

I saw there were inset cupboards under the seating. I knelt down. What would be inside? I reached out my hand to open one. And froze. There was a creaking of wood from outside. My heart pounded. I stood up quickly.

The door slowly opened. I put my hands to my mouth to stifle a scream. I wished I'd never come exploring.

A man entered. He was taken aback to see me there. I recognised him. It was Arthur Sankey, the policeman who'd been coming to Muirfield regularly. This was the first time I'd seen him up close. I let out a breath I'd been holding. I felt sure he'd do me no harm.

'What are you doing here?' he demanded. 'Identify yourself immediately.'

'Hannah Miller, sir.' I dipped a curtsey and lowered my gaze.

'Hannah Miller? I've seen you before. You're a maid at the Hall, aren't you? What are you doing here in the summerhouse?'

That was a very good question. And one to which I didn't want to give the true answer. I could hardly say I was trying to do his job and catch a murderer. Instead I played the foolish girl.

'Oh, sir, I wanted to feed the ducks.'

Since the ducks were a good long distance off on the far side of the lake, and I was in the middle of the summerhouse with the door shut, it was not the best answer I could've managed. However, he didn't challenge me. Instead, with a frown and a swipe of his fingers along his profuse moustache, he advised me to return to the house.

'This isn't the time to be wandering alone on the grounds. There's a murderer on the loose, don't you know?

'Oh, yes, sir. It was silly of me.' I blinked.

He harrumphed and puffed out his chest importantly. His brass buttons were shined to gold. His belt was neat and doing a fine job of keeping in his belly.

'No matter. We'll say no more about it. But you must go back to the house now. I'm interviewing all the staff.'

'Again?' It was cheeky, but the words were out of my mouth before I filtered them.

He stared at me. 'A girl's gone missing from the village. It's very likely she's met with the same fate as Ellen. Hurry along now, and stick to the path.'

I brushed past him and left the summerhouse. At the edge of the trees, my foot on the start of the path, I turned. He was looking at me, his portly figure on the wooden platform.

The lake as his backdrop was sombre. The rain had stopped, but the mist of droplets lingered.

★　★　★

In the end, I was interviewed too. The house was in an uproar. Mrs Smith was tense, two lines bracketing her lips as she told us all that the policeman wanted to talk to us. Mrs Pearson was complaining about her crockery. She needed to put it back in her cupboards. She'd no time to be interviewed. Sure, hadn't she told Mr Sankey everything she knew already — which was nothing! Janet was crying. No one knew why. Gracie looked worried. If Arthur Sankey was taking May Litton's disappearance seriously, then she felt at any moment she could be called home. Mr Joseph vanished into his room. I guessed he was shifting bottles of wine in his cupboard so his theft wouldn't be uncovered. Only Bill was calm.

'I don't know why Mr Sankey wants

to talk to me,' I said as we stood in the corridor waiting. 'I wasn't here when Ellen was killed.'

'Don't be nervous,' Bill said. 'It's probably routine.'

'Look, Bill,' I said slowly, 'the other day . . .'

'Don't mention it,' he said. 'Really, it was nothing.'

I felt oddly lost and slightly flattened. So he hadn't been bothered whether I went to the tea room with him or not. Probably he only asked because Sarah wasn't free. Anyway, I didn't care either. I had Adam to think about. But it continued to rankle. I glanced at him. His features were solemn. He wasn't bad-looking, I thought. He had a kind face. His jaw was square and strong. He was very tall, like all good footmen ought to be. There was a slight gangliness to him that was endearing. I stopped there.

'Well, can we be friends?' I asked.

A rare smile lit his face. 'Aye, friends it is then.'

I smiled too.

'Hannah Miller,' Arthur Sankey's booming voice called me in.

* * *

The policeman had been given over Mrs Smith's own room for use. I'd been in it only once, the day I arrived at Muirfield Hall. The furnishings were plain but good quality. It was warm, with a fire lit in the hearth and a stack of logs ready to add to it. A brass bucket of coal stood there too, and a hook of poker, tongs and brush. All was neat and perfect. Just like Mrs Smith herself.

'Did you know May Litton?' Arthur Sankey asked. He had a notebook and pen at the ready. He rested it on his stomach as he sat in the only armchair. I stood before him and was not offered a seat.

'No, I never met her.'

'Did you know Ellen Munroe?'

'No, she died before I came to Muirfield,' I told him.

'Where did you come from?' the policeman asked, taking notes.

'A county over.'

I described where my parents' cottage was and the farming community they belonged to. He nodded. He obviously knew the place.

'And lastly, Hannah, have you noticed anything unusual since you got here?'

'I don't know what you mean exactly, sir.'

He waved an arm in the air. 'People acting strangely, bumps in the night and so forth.'

Then it struck me. He didn't have a clue. Literally. He was no closer to solving Ellen's murder than I was. He was grasping for straws, and May Litton's disappearance was such a straw. When I didn't speak, he grunted.

'That will be all for now.'

6

A Beautiful Flower

Every part of Muirfield apparently needed to be taken apart and cleaned. Not a rug or carpet was left unturned. The picture frames gleamed. The skirting shone. The chandeliers were carefully lowered so that each individual crystal drop could be gently washed and dried. The air smelt sweet and lemony. The best beeswax candles were placed in sconces and candlesticks to supplement the gas lighting.

Janet was put to work by Mrs Pearson to clean all the pots and pans, bowls and cake tins in preparation for the cooking ahead. They were already clean, but poor Janet had to do them again. The cook watched with a frown. It was a serious business.

For my part, my task was unexpected.

Mrs Smith drew me to one side. 'Hannah, you must put on a clean apron and tidy your hair. You're needed upstairs to help Sarah prepare the young ladies' dresses. I know it's unusual, but Mrs Dawton is taking up all of Sarah's time. We've a small staff here and I can't see any other way round it.'

She sounded tired. It made me think. It was all very well having a shooting party, but there was no thought from the Dawtons to the extra work burden placed upon their servants. We had no voice in the matter. If my mother had heard my thoughts, I knew what she would say. It's not our place to argue. We're lucky to be paid and to work.

While I was grateful for my job at Muirfield, I didn't see why I should work like a slave. I didn't warm to Mrs Dawton. She had no feeling for her maids, that was certain. In any case, I nodded to the housekeeper. 'Yes, Mrs Smith. I'll go directly.'

'You're a good girl.' She smiled and patted my arm.

I was pleased. It warmed me that she thought well of me. I felt I'd settled in and was amongst friends. With a light heart, I changed my uniform and went upstairs. But Sarah soon put a stop to my happiness.

'Oh, it's you. What are you doing up here?'

'Mrs Smith sent me to help you. I've to lay out the young ladies' dresses.'

'I *can* manage.'

'In that case, I'll go back downstairs.' I made as if to leave.

'Wait!'

I paused.

'Maybe there are some tasks I can set you,' she said haughtily.

I had to admire her spirit. She was making it quite clear who was boss. As lady's maid, she was higher in the rankings than me, and she wanted me to know it.

'Let's get started then,' I replied with a smile.

Her green eyes flashed with anger. She didn't like me talking back. But she needed me. She might not like to admit it, but there was too much for her to do that day. I didn't want to work with her either, but there it was; neither of us had a say in it. Sarah didn't dare send me back down. She'd have had to face the wrath of Mrs Smith, who I'd no doubt could be terrifying if necessary.

'Come along.' She swept in front of me, as hoity-toity as a lady. Airs and graces learned from her mistress, I suspected.

I followed her along the corridor until we reached a beautiful wide room. This was Miss Alice's bedroom. Miss Alice was there. She turned a sulky face to us at our arrival. She was very like her mother — the same dark wavy hair and unkind blue eyes. Her full mouth curved in dissatisfaction with life. Across the vast bed lay piles of materials. There were day dresses, evening dresses, stoles, scarves, bodices and stockings of every colour and shade. Cotton, linen, silks and velvets. I drew in a silent breath. What wealth there was in this one display.

'Do hurry up, Murray. I don't have all day.' Even the imperious tone sounded just like Mrs Dawton. Her sixteen-year-old daughter had learned plenty from her mother.

Sarah curtseyed. 'Yes, miss. This is Hannah, who will help you with your dress.'

'Why can't you?' Now her voice was querulous.

'I have to help your mother now. But I'll be back as quick as I can, miss.'

And I was left with a stroppy young lady. Unsure what a lady's maid actually did, I began by tidying the piles into some order. Alice watched me for a while. I tried not to be unsettled by her glare. Then she threw herself into an armchair.

'What should I wear?'

'What colours do you like?' This was a good place to begin.

She looked surprised. 'I don't know. Murray lays out my clothes each day.'

'Well, there's a very pretty green

velvet dress here. Or perhaps you'd like this navy silk?'

She got up from the armchair. Nonchalantly, she drifted to the bed. I smoothed out the dresses for her to see. Idly, she pointed at the navy silk. It was a beautiful creation with a neat waist and delicate needlework at the cuffs and neckline. 'That's a good choice, miss,' I said.

A hint of a smile touched her mouth before the spoilt expression returned. She shrugged. 'I don't care what I wear. Leave it there. And find me the matching stuff.'

'There's a pretty shawl to go with it.' I held up a long, slim silk shawl. It would be perfect draped over her shoulders.

'Yes, that is nice.' She sat on the bed near me, beginning to look interested.

The door was pushed open and Emily came in. She smiled when she saw me. 'Hello, Hannah. How are you?'

'I'm very well, Miss Emily. And you?'

She skipped around the room. 'I'm

very excited, Hannah. Very excited. There's going to be a party.'

Her enthusiasm made me laugh. At that, Alice frowned. She spun round to look at her little sister. 'Get out! You're such a nuisance. You'll mess my things up. You always do.'

Emily didn't seem put out. She was perhaps used to this from her sister. She skipped out the door with a wave to me.

'That wasn't very nice of you, miss,' I said.

'You can get out too,' she shouted. 'Leave me alone.'

I curtseyed politely and left. I'd sorted her clothes. If she wanted to brush her own hair, that was fine by me.

Sarah came running along the corridor. 'What now?'

'I've organised Miss Alice's clothes and she asked me to leave.'

She glared at me. 'You've hardly been in there half an hour.'

'I could help Miss Emily,' I suggested. That would be a happier job by leaps and bounds.

She shook her head. 'No, I've done that. Mrs Dawton wants me to do her hair now in the new French style. I need more pins.'

I gave a half shrug. It wasn't my problem. If Sarah had been a nicer person, I'd have attempted to help her. But she'd made it plain she didn't like me. It was mutual. Her behaviour to Janet had been atrocious. As far as I was concerned, she could find her own pins.

Did some of this show on my face? Because she stiffened, ready to lash out. 'You're not the first to be taken in by his handsome face,' she said.

I stepped back involuntarily. There was pure acid in her voice. I knew at once she meant Adam. How did she know? Had she been watching me? The views from the upstairs storey of the house were good.

'I'm not blind,' she went on. 'None of us are. There are no secrets in this house.'

And I thought how wrong she was. For it came upon me then what a place of secrets Muirfield Hall was. It harboured someone evil, I was convinced of it. Whoever killed Ellen was here. Now. I didn't believe it was an outsider, or an opportunist. No; Ellen had upset someone here. 'I don't know what you're talking about,' I said.

She threw me a look of scorn. 'That's right; deny it, then, if you will. But I'll bet you didn't know that Ellen and Adam were stepping out. That's news to you, isn't it?'

I was too stunned to answer. I felt dizzy as I stepped away from her. I went down the stairs, barely seeing them. Sarah's arrow had pierced the spot. Ellen and Adam? Could it be true? Why hadn't Gracie told me this? More to the point, why hadn't Adam?

* * *

I had no more time to ponder Sarah's words, as downstairs all was a bustling chaos. There were noises and people everywhere. The Dawtons' guests had arrived along with their many servants. Mrs Smith looked tense as she instructed them where to put their belongings. Upstairs, I knew that Mr Joseph was welcoming the family's guests.

Bill stopped beside me. 'What a commotion. Who'd have believed three couples would need all this lot?' He gestured to the strangers milling about in the servants' hall. Well, they were strangers to me, but they were chatting with Gracie and Janet, who appeared to know them.

'Such a lot of people,' I agreed, smiling up at him. I was glad that he and I were now friends.

'I heard you were upstairs helping Sarah.' His expression was neutral.

'Yes, that's right. Not for long, though.' I thought of Sarah's parting sting.

He grinned. What a nice face he had when it lit up like that. 'She won't like you on her territory.'

I laughed, thinking it a fine description, as if Sarah was a prowling tiger on the floor above us. It suited her tawny hair. 'No, she didn't like it much,' I agreed, 'but Mrs Smith sent me up and there was much to do. I helped Miss Alice choose her dress.'

'She's a handful, Miss Alice,' Bill remarked. 'Unlike Miss Emily, who's a little ray of sunshine in this gloomy house.'

Before I could answer, he had moved on, one of the other footmen asking him for advice. Then Gracie was clutching my elbow.

'Look,' she whispered loudly. 'Look, over there.'

I followed the line of her sight. There was a young man, really a grown boy, standing there. He was laden with luggage. Mrs Smith was pointing to the servants' stairs. He was thin with brown, tufted hair and prominent ears.

'Is that your Johnny?' I asked, already sure it was by the way Gracie turned a pretty shade of pink.

'That's him,' she sighed. 'Isn't he gorgeous?'

'He's . . . Yes, he is that.' I hugged her.

She giggled. 'He's asked me to dance with him tomorrow night at the servants' party.'

'There'll be dancing?'

'Of course. There'll be lots of food and drink and music and dancing. I can't wait. It's going to be such fun. You'll enjoy it.'

I wondered if Adam would be there. I imagined us dancing together. It gave me a shiver right along my spine.

'How does that work then? Surely Mr Joseph and Bill have to wait on the guests?'

'There's shooting during the day, and we have to bring out the food for when the men get back,' Gracie explained. 'Then while the men are shooting, the ladies will want tea and cakes and will play cards. In the evening they have dinner of course. But after that, we get our own party, and Cook lays out a cold buffet for the Dawtons and their visitors that they help themselves to. It's a tradition every year.'

She squeezed my arm and left, Mrs Smith calling her to help. I went into the kitchen, where it was quieter. Mrs Pearson was puffing, red-faced, as she lifted out a large tray of breads.

'Hannah, you stay here and get these cooled off. There's two pheasant pies to come out of the oven in five minutes, too. They're having a grand dinner tonight before the hunting tomorrow. I have to go and see Mrs Dawton about the menu.'

'Isn't it rather late?' I said.

'She's changed her mind about dessert,' Mrs Pearson said, sounding very annoyed. 'I had them all made and now I'm going to have to start all over again.'

She rushed out of the kitchen. I sat before the hot oven, ready to take out the pies. There was a wonderful smell of game and gravy and hot pastry.

'Hello, here you are.' Miss Emily danced into the room.

'Should you be here, miss?' I cautioned. 'Won't your mama miss you?'

'She doesn't want her friends to see me,' Emily said, 'so I came to see Cook.'

I was shocked. Did Emily believe that? Or had she overheard her mother say so? Was she not to be introduced to the guests? She was an odd sort of girl, and I could quite imagine her not measuring up to Mrs Dawton's ideals. If it was true, it made Mrs Dawton a very cold woman indeed.

'Cook had to run upstairs, but she'll be back soon,' I said. 'Do you want to wait here with me?'

'Oh yes, please, Hannah,' Emily said as if it was a gift I was handing her.

I remembered the pies. I lifted them out of the oven carefully. The steam rose up and dampened my face. The pastry was flaky and golden and perfect. Mrs Pearson was a great cook.

'Oh no, this won't do. This won't do at all,' Mrs Pearson said as she appeared, flapping her hands.

Both Emily and I were startled. I glanced at the pies. Was there something wrong with them? But it was Emily she meant.

'Come along, Miss Emily. Your father's looking for you.'

Emily jumped up happily. 'Where is Papa?'

'Run straight upstairs and find him,' Cook said, giving the girl a little push.

Emily trotted away. Mrs Pearson shook her head darkly.

'She'll get herself into trouble someday. Head in the clouds. Not a jot of common sense.'

'But a nice child,' I said, quick to defend her.

'A very nice little girl,' Mrs Pearson said with a nod. 'But she doesn't belong down here. Just as much as we don't belong up there.'

With those sage words, she turned her attention to the pies.

When Cook wasn't watching, I slipped outside. A breath of fresh air was what I needed. Adam came round the corner. My heart jolted. I didn't expect to see him at the house. It was like seeing a fish out of water. He was associated in my mind with the gardeners' bothy and the walled garden.

'Will you come with me?' he said without surprise, as if he knew I'd be there.

I glanced back at the kitchen door. I should not. There were many tasks to be done. Mrs Smith and Mrs Pearson would want me soon. And yet . . . I couldn't bear to say no to him. So I nodded smartly.

'Where are we going?'

He didn't answer so I walked along with him, thrilled he was there. I managed sideways looks, drinking in his handsome face, the way his necktie showed off his tanned skin and the way his shoulder muscles strained against his cotton shirt.

He took me back from the house, beyond the bothy and the row of cottages. We were heading for the summerhouse. There was no one around. I guessed that was why we were going there. All the activity was at the house itself as the visitors settled in for the festivities ahead.

'It's a beautiful day,' I ventured.

'Aye.'

The breeze rustled in the trees. As we passed, the leaves dropped in ones and twos. The ground was carpeted with yellow, orange and burnt brown hues of autumn. It was soft beneath my feet, like sinking into a luxurious carpet.

The lake was shimmering with ripples from the wind. The ducks were far out in the middle, a circle of bobbing black shapes. The place seemed less depressing than my last visit. Even the fringe of vegetation on the edge of the lake didn't make me shudder. I kept clear of it, though. Following Adam's lead, I climbed onto the wooden platform and then into the summerhouse.

'It's quiet here,' he said by way of explanation.

'Nice to be away from all the noise,' I said, waiting. Why were we here?

'I want to give you this.' He pushed something into my hands. It was dry and papery. I looked down. It was a single flower. I didn't know what kind. It had a sturdy green stem and a yellow centre. The petals were white and frilly. I lifted it to my nose and inhaled. A faint scent, sweet as vanilla, came to me.

'It's lovely,' I said.

'It's for you.' He coughed and stared away out at the lake through the small window.

'Thank you. I'll treasure it always.' And I would. I'd press it between the pages of my book so it'd last forever. My heart was singing. He liked me. More than liked me. I saw a future with him. But first, I had to ask him . . . 'Were you and Ellen courting?'

He recoiled. 'Who told you that?'

'Sarah Murray.'

116

He mumbled something under his breath.

'Adam? It doesn't matter to me, I don't know why I asked.' I wished to take my foolish question back, seeing his annoyance. I'd spoiled our romantic moment.

'She liked me, that's all. She and I were never an item. Sarah's a meddlesome maid.' He strode out of the summerhouse and I ran to the door to follow him and to apologise. But then I hesitated. Here was my chance to see what was in the inset cupboards under the seating. Then I could chase after Adam.

I knelt swiftly and pulled at the nearest knob handle. The cupboard door flung open. I ducked down to see. There was nothing. It was empty. Rapidly, I pulled them all open. But all were empty. Then I remembered Adam. I pushed them shut and pulled myself up. Almost tripping on my long skirts, I reached the door and ran out.

Adam was standing at the edge of the

wood, staring in my direction, just like the day I'd met the policeman. Except then I'd been at the woods, and Mr Sankey had been here on the platform.

As I hurried onto the path, Adam turned and walked into the woods. A petal drifted from my precious flower and landed on the ground. Holding it carefully, I walked as fast as possible back to Muirfield.

7

The House Party

The gentlemen had all risen early and gone hunting. There was much male laughter and talk as they left with servants, guns and dogs accompanying them. The morning for us was dull. There was the usual cleaning to be done, fires to be made up and vegetables to be scrubbed. I wanted to ask Gracie about Adam and Ellen, but I never got the chance. She was upstairs and I was kept in the kitchen much of the while.

Eventually, Mrs Smith called for me to take up tea and cakes to Mrs Dawton and her visitors. I put on a fresh apron and took the tray. The ladies were in the pretty living room overlooking the front of the house. There were five of them, including my employer. Their day dresses were a rainbow of silks spread over the sofas and armchairs, and the room was filled with sweet perfumes.

Carefully, I laid down the silver tray. I took the teapot and poured five cups. They chinked on their matching saucers. I prayed I wouldn't spill a drop, or worse, break a delicate cup. The porcelain was so thin.

I managed somehow. The dainty cakes were Mrs Pearson's best effort. There were vanilla sponges, chocolate and ginger. All were iced with tiny decorations. It made my mouth water to see them. I hoped that Cook had some left over for the servants' lunch.

'Don't you find it dreary in the countryside?' one lady asked innocently of her hostess.

Mrs Dawton's lips tightened before she managed a smile. 'Oh, it's pleasant enough when we have company, which we often do. And of course, Herbert and I are planning to acquire a town house in Glasgow in the spring.'

There was a ruffle of silk and ribbons at this comment. It was news to me. So was the fact that they often had company here. It wasn't my impression. I decided I'd ask Gracie about that too, when I caught up with her.

I stood silently, waiting as I'd been taught, in case I was needed further. Luckily, I wasn't dismissed immediately. I could eavesdrop shamelessly.

'How marvellous,' a slim lady with looped brown hair said. 'Will you live there? I suppose you will move your staff to town.'

'Very likely.' Mrs Dawton nodded, as if thinking about this herself. 'Yes indeed, that's what we will do. So much nicer to be in the city. We can visit Muirfield out of season.'

I felt a pang of dismay while my face stayed still. I had to pretend I was deaf and blind to do my job properly. I had no desire to live in Glasgow. I wasn't a city girl. It would be so far from home. I tried to imagine Gracie and Bill and even little Janet coping in the city, and failed.

At that moment, Mrs Dawton noticed

me. With a frown, she waved me off. 'That will be all.'

I went quietly from the room. Nothing endeared me to Mrs Dawton. Every time I met her, I disliked her more.

I hurried along the corridor, trying to outrace my thoughts. I nearly had a heart attack when Emily jumped out in front of me. Pressing my hand to my chest, I scolded her. 'Oh, Miss Emily, what a shock you gave me. Why are you hiding in there, waiting to scare me?'

Her face crumpled. 'I didn't mean to scare you, Hannah. It was a joke. I like hiding. I can hear people. They say things they wouldn't say if they saw me.'

I stared at her. Miss Emily was part of the secrets of the house. What had she overheard, sneaking about?

'That's not a good idea,' I told her. 'You'll not hear good about yourself if you listen in when you're not meant to.' Then I thought how insincere I was, having just listened in to Emily's mother's conversations! I could hardly condemn Emily for something I'd found useful myself.

'They never saw me,' she said with a cunning look.

'Who?' I said, already thinking about the work waiting for me downstairs and not really concentrating on the child in front of me.

'It doesn't matter. You don't like me. You're like the others.'

Now I took notice of her. There were tears forming in her big blue eyes. 'Now, Miss Emily, that's not true. I do like you very much.'

She brightened. What a mercurial creature she was. 'I like you too, Hannah.'

'What did you mean that the others don't like you? What others?' I asked.

She found sudden interest in the tassels on her dress. She twisted them in her fingers. '*She* didn't like me. She pinched me on the arm.'

'That wasn't nice of her. Tell me her name.' Was this real, or was Emily's imagination taking over? She had a rich internal life, I could tell. Most lonely children did.

'She got punished. She deserved it.' For a fleeting moment, an expression slid over the child's face that made me shiver.

'What are you talking about?' I wanted to grab her arms and shake the truth out of her.

She stepped back at my sharp tone. The tassels on her dress were limp. She stuck her fingers into her mouth and chewed at her nails. I realised I'd get no more sense from her. I dipped a curtsey. 'Well, miss, I must get on with my duties.'

I skirted past her, uneasy in some way. As I reached the top of the back service stairs, she shouted after me.

'She died. That's what happened.'

I gasped and turned back. Was she talking about Ellen? If so, I wanted to know more. I was in time to see the soles of her soft slippers and the white froth of her petticoats as she fled to her room.

The gentlemen returned much later, surrounded by the smells of mud and blood and gunpowder. It was a bright, dry day, and we were to take food outside to a long trestle table. They wanted to play at picnics. There was a shelter with seats behind the trestle. I met with Gracie as we hurried to settle the picnic on the table. It looked enticing. There was a red and white cloth to hide the rough wood. There were flagons of wine and beer. The centrepiece was a grand raised pork pie with honey glazing. Then there were thick, good bread and churned butter, blackberry jams and other delicious things.

I saw then why it was an outside affair. Firstly, they were hungry from their exertions. They wouldn't want to take the time to clean up, change clothes and eat in a civilised way. Secondly, their blood was still up from the chase — that was clear in the pitch of their voices and their bragging. A nausea welled up in me at the sight of the limp bodies of rabbits and pheasants slung over the menservants' shoulders. These were laid in a line along the gravel path. *Poor things*, I thought.

'It's a sorry sight,' someone spoke behind me. It was Bill.

I nodded. 'I don't like to see them. It's horrible.' I liked him all the better for his sympathy towards the animals.

'But they'll taste good,' he said with a grin, 'so it's not all in vain.'

I found myself smiling back at him. His grin was infectious somehow. It brought a crease to his cheek in a charming way. 'Your face is muddy,' I said.

He swiped at it with his sleeve. 'Not a wonder, since I've been dragged through the hedgerows and brambles, beating for this lot. It's tiring, flushing up the beasts.'

'I suppose so. Not as dull as taking tea to the ladies though,' I said pertly.

'Don't tell me you'd rather be beating for the gentlemen, 'cause I won't believe that.'

'I'd much rather be outdoors and feel the wind on my face than stuck in all day,' I told him with feeling.

'Well, you're out now,' he reminded me.

'Will you eat?'

'I daresay Mrs Pearson will have something set for us lads.' He touched his cap to me and went on his way.

I marvelled at how our friendship had blossomed. He no longer seemed the grumpy, unfriendly sort I'd tagged him as. I began to see what Sarah was attracted to in him. Not that I felt that way myself. My attraction was all for Adam. I hugged the image of the flower he'd given me to my heart. He loved me, I was sure of it. And I loved him too. I was ready to wed, and I thought perhaps the Dawtons might give us married quarters on the estate. There were empty cottages, I knew that from the servants' talk. One of those would be perfect. I saw us there, growing old and contented in each other's company. I'd have my sister Kitty come to stay.

She might even get work here. She'd do light laundry or take in sewing just as she did at home.

I was humming a little tune, happy with my plans as I sorted the provisions and poured beer. The gentlemen swooped in and took the offered plates of food and the great big glasses of drinks. They stood, exchanging tall tales of the morning's chase of small animals. Around their legs, the dogs wandered or flopped on stiff paws watching their masters. The servants had gone back into the house, their duties never stopping.

Gracie nudged me. 'Someone's happy. What's with you today?'

'I can't be happy with my work?' I teased. 'Shame on you.'

She laughed. 'It's more than that. Go on, tell me.'

But I didn't want to share my news about Adam. Not yet. I wanted to wrap it around me and keep it secret. Besides, there were things I needed to hear from Gracie.

'You're quite jolly yourself,' I deflected

her. 'Is it your Johnny?'

She tossed her head, pleased. 'I do like seeing him. That's the truth. I can't wait to dance with him.'

I tried to sound casual as I prepared my next question. There was no need for Gracie to see how hurt I was. 'I heard something about Adam.'

'What was that then?' Gracie filled up the flagons again and cut more pork pie. The food was going down rapidly, with no signs of the gentlemen stopping eating.

'Only that Ellen had a fancy for him.' I believed Adam's story. Sarah had reason to lie to me about them stepping out.

Gracie looked uncomfortable.

'Why didn't you tell me?' I asked. 'You must've guessed how I feel about him.'

'Everyone's guessed,' she said.

'Is it a problem?' I asked nervously. If Mrs Smith disapproved, I could lose my position.

She shook her head. 'I don't think so.

But then neither was Ellen and Adam courting. We all thought they'd get married eventually. Not that they told anyone that. It was a slow sort of stepping out. Adam's not the sort to be impulsive.'

'They were courting? I thought . . . I was told that Ellen liked Adam but he didn't feel the same way.'

Gracie looked at me, 'Who told you that? No, they were quite the lovebirds for a while. Then, as I say, it cooled off a bit, but it was bound to end in a wedding. Only, she died.'

I couldn't believe it. I didn't want to. Why had Adam lied to me?

'Hannah, you've gone quite white. Are you all right?'

No, I was not all right. I was deeply confused and mixed up. I could no longer tell what was true and what was false. Nor who to trust.

'By the way,' Gracie said, 'May Litton's turned up. My mother is very relieved, and so am I, for my own selfish reasons.'

'That is good. Which means that there is no murderer stalking unsuspecting girls.'

'But that doesn't bring Ellen back.'

'Where was May Litton?'

'She won't say, but I'd bet my best hat there was a man involved.' Gracie grinned. 'The good news is, my mother has calmed down for now. She's still worried about me working here, but she's not grumbling for me to leave right away.'

*   *   *

'You'll be serving at dinner tonight,' Mrs Smith announced later. 'Mr Joseph and Bill need an extra pair of hands, what with all the visitors. Muirfield must not be seen to be wanting in any aspect.'

I was quite excited at the prospect. I had some small experience of serving meals from working for the Collingtons. They had occasionally asked me to help with lunches. Mind you, they had a larger staff, and my main duties had been looking after Arthur. Still, I reckoned I'd do okay.

'Don't worry,' Bill said, coming over to me after Mrs Smith had gone, 'I'll keep you right.'

'Thanks. Will it be formal?'

'The evening meal will be formal with Mr Joseph overseeing it,' Bill said. 'But once we're having our party, there will be a buffet and the upstairs folks will help themselves. It'll be nice to have some hours to ourselves, not at their beck and call.'

'Don't you like being a footman?' There had been a bitter note in his voice.

'Does anyone like being in service?' he parried.

'I never thought much about it,' I said. 'There's no alternative. At least, not for girls like me.'

'Girls like you.' Bill's gaze flickered over me. 'I don't think there are any other girls like you.'

'Now you're being daft,' I pushed

him playfully. 'There's nothing special about me. Away with you.'

He looked as if he'd say more, then grinned and went off. It was odd, but I began to sense there were layers to him. As his friend, I wanted to find out more. Perhaps at the servants' party that night, I would.

* * *

I admit I was nervous that evening, standing ready to go upstairs with a tureen of soup in my hands. Bill and Mr Joseph were already gone.

'Hurry up, hurry up!' Mrs Pearson shouted, flapping her hands at me as if I was a stray chicken. 'The soup will get cold with you hovering there. Get going.'

I clutched the tureen as if my life depended on it and went upstairs. I tried to remember Mr Joseph's quick instructions. He'd snapped them out, distracted by his own tasks. All I could remember was not to speak, not to lean over the guests, and definitely not to spill the soup!

Despite my nerves, I enjoyed it. All I had to do was set the soup tureen on the sideboard for Bill to serve. Mr Joseph poured the wine. The guests were chatty and didn't care who gave them their food as long as they got some, or so it appeared. Mrs Dawton's flinty eyes darted towards us, but she was soon taken up in conversation by the gentleman next to her.

I stood as I'd been instructed, back to the wall, waiting to be ordered about, my face blank. I was able to observe all that went on. What fun it was. I focused on Mr Dawton's voice. He was stroking his bristling whiskers and telling his listeners about his plants. My senses prickled when I heard Adam's name.

'He's a fine gardener. I'm lucky to have him. He can make anything grow. Why, if I get a special package of seeds from America, he can take those fellows and within months I have a collection of plants worth a pocketful of gold.

There is not a garden in Scotland that can match Muirfield's for variety and exotic species.'

His dining companions looked suitably impressed. So was I. I'd no idea the plants were so valuable. A pocketful of gold — really? That was interesting. I was proud to hear Adam's praises being sung by Mr Dawton. I was going to be marrying an important man. There was no doubt in my mind now that we'd get a cottage if Adam asked.

★   ★   ★

Later, it was the party we'd all been waiting for. Cook and Janet had created a lovely buffet for the family upstairs. Gracie and I helped to lay it all out.

'It's traditional, you see,' Mrs Pearson said when she saw me staring. 'It's only this once in the year. They help themselves and we get the evening off. And don't you worry, there'll be plenty of good food for us tonight too. I've been working hard for this day.'

'You've done a wonderful job,' I said, and was rewarded with her beaming face.

Gracie and I went up to our room to change. I had one decent dress. It was a pretty shade of blue, like a summer evening sky. The wrists and collar had a tiny tracing of lace, and I knew it flattered me. I had no slippers and had to be content with my laced boots. They wouldn't be visible under my hems, I hoped.

'You look beautiful,' Gracie sighed when I'd got ready.

'This is a hand-me-down from Mrs Collington, my previous employer,' I explained. 'Luckily she was about my size, and very generous with her cast-offs. I don't have a shawl quality enough to go with it, but I'll manage. You look very nice too.'

Gracie wore a dove-grey gown. It was plain, but clean and serviceable. I didn't ask but guessed it too was a cast-off, perhaps from the church collections. It wasn't as if Gracie's family had money for good clothes.

I shook out my hair into a softer style and threw my cap on the bed. Gracie did the same, and we laughed in our freedom.

'Let's go and enjoy the party,' Gracie said, linking arms with me and pulling me along with her.

Downstairs, the Muirfield staff and the visiting servants were milling about. The table and chairs had been pushed to one side of the room. Mrs Pearson, true to her word, had set out a feast. Gracie and I picked up plates and joined the queue. I glanced about for Adam. Surely he'd come? He knew I'd be there. I couldn't see him yet.

Someone had a fiddle and began to play. At once, couples formed and a dance started. It was cramped enough, but no one seemed to care. I stared about, looking for that familiar face.

'He won't come,' Bill said in my ear. 'He never does. Will you dance with me? I'm a poor substitute, I know, but we're friends after all.'

I hesitated. Bill had cleaned up well. Out of his footman's uniform he looked older, more confident. It would be churlish to refuse a dance. So I nodded, and he took my hands and led me onto the dance floor. The tempo of the fiddle picked up. It was a country dance and one I knew well. It required gusto, stomping feet and whooping. I let it all out, felt myself laughing, felt myself free. Bill's shining eyes caught mine. For a while I forgot Adam and let the dance engulf me.

8

Following Mrs Smith

A few days later, the visitors had gone. The house was very quiet without the gaiety of the outings, card games, piano recitals and other entertainments that had gone on. I had enjoyed meeting new people and being out of the daily routines of the house; we all had. But I had something to do. It was soon to be Mrs Smith's afternoon off — I heard her discussing it with Mr Joseph — and this time I was going to follow her properly. I had my day off too. I had neglected my hunt for Ellen's killer. Now I'd push forward by finding out what Mrs Smith had to hide.

I made my way down the driveway and round the curve of it. There ahead of me was the gatehouse. There was no sign of Mrs Smith yet. I had made sure

I was out of the house before her. Once I reached the gatehouse, I turned left. There was the wagon, just I had hoped. The horse was grazing on the grass lazily. The driver was chewing on a doorstop of bread. He stopped when he saw me.

'Good afternoon,' I said with a bright smile. 'Where are you headed to today?'

He took off his cap and named a market town. I knew of it, although I'd never been there. It was on the route back to my own home. I had passed through it with Mr Dawton on my way to Muirfield.

'That's where I'm going.' I pretended to be surprised. 'Can you take an extra passenger?'

He named his price. I had some money, having planned in advance. Most of my wages were sent home, but I had enough put by. So far, there had been nothing to spend it on. My days off were for reading or walking into the village with Gracie.

I paid the driver and climbed up into

the wagon. It was a bare sort of vehicle, with no comforts on the wooden seat. I folded my coat-tails under me for padding and warmth. My breath was white puffs. I tucked my fingers into my sleeves, wishing I had a good pair of gloves.

Then round the corner came Mrs Smith. She stopped dead when she saw me. Then she quickly recovered and arrived at the wagon with a polite smile. She wore her habitual black coat and wide black hat. In her hand was her long umbrella.

'Mrs Smith,' I said, 'I do hope you don't mind me joining you? I have an aunt to visit, and the wagon is going to the right place.'

Some sort of turmoil showed in her expression before she nodded. 'Of course. I'll be glad of the company on such a cold day.' She climbed up and sat opposite me.

The driver clicked at his horse and pulled on the reins until it lifted its head from the ground. The horse snorted and whinnied. Then obediently it began to move off. The wagon swayed before settling into a rhythm. I quite enjoyed travelling along and seeing the world go by. Mrs Smith offered no conversation, and I didn't know what to say. So I contented myself with watching the countryside.

I could almost forget why I was there. It was a lovely day to be out. Although cold, there was no breeze. The trees were beautiful colours, some bare-branched now. I saw a squirrel leap from one tree to another. In the sky were trails of birds, heading somewhere with purpose. Like me. I must have purpose. It was no day trip really. I wanted to solve the mystery of where Mrs Smith went on her afternoons off. In that way, I hoped to find out whether there could be any connection with Ellen's death.

'Why is it up to you to solve?' Gracie had asked a few days ago.

We were up in our attic room at night, both lying awake in our narrow beds. There's something vulnerable about life at those hours. It's a time when truth and worries and fears abound. I had confessed to my search for Ellen Munroe's murderer. Gracie was perplexed.

'It isn't right that there's a murderer going about his or her life, getting away with such a hideous crime.' I pulled my covers closer to me.

'It's wrong,' Gracie agreed, 'but that doesn't make it your job to find out who it is.'

'Mr Sankey hasn't made much progress,' I reminded her.

'We don't know that. He's not going to tell the likes of us, is he? For all we know, he's on his way right now to get the culprit.'

'Unlikely.'

'Well, anyway,' she sighed, and I heard the creak of her bedsprings as she rolled over, 'it's a dangerous idea, what you're doing. What if the murderer finds out you're looking for him?'

'I'm being very careful. I don't see how he could. Or she. It doesn't have to be a man. That edge to the lake is very slippery. It wouldn't need much strength to push someone in.'

'That's horrible.' There was a pause, then she sprang up in her bed. 'I can help you. We'll be detectives together.'

I didn't want to put Gracie in any danger, so I was reluctant to include her. But she was insistent. 'Very well then,' I said. 'The most important thing you can do is wrack your brains for any unusual goings on in the weeks leading up to Ellen's death.'

'I can keep my ears open too,' she replied eagerly. 'I hear all sorts of nonsense upstairs. Maids are invisible to the family.'

Why hadn't I thought of the family as suspects? Here was me telling Gracie she shouldn't get involved, when almost instantly she'd pointed out something enormous that I'd missed. The Dawtons. But what reason was there for them to kill Ellen? Same as any other, was the answer. She had known something — something so important she wasn't to be allowed to tell it. I was certain of that. It fitted what I had heard about her personality. She liked to know people's business and use it against them. Sarah and Bill, for example. But who else?

'Gracie,' I urged, 'did Ellen seem to have a hold over anyone?'

'Do you mean like when she told Bill about Sarah?'

'Yes, like that.' I was pleased at Gracie's quick wits.

She leaned on her elbow, facing me and frowning as she thought about it. 'I do remember a strange atmosphere between her and Mr Joseph. She didn't get on well with Mrs Smith, either.'

'Tell me,' I demanded.

'It was more a feeling I got than anything solid. Just that she got away with stuff that wouldn't be tolerated in me or the other servants. She was . . . cheeky. Like she knew she could say it and not lose her place.'

'Could she have been blackmailing them?' I spoke aloud without realising it.

Gracie was shocked. 'Oh no, that's

going too far. Isn't it?'

'I don't know. Even if she knew things about them that they didn't want others to find out, I suppose that would be enough to give her power over them.'

'She wasn't all bad,' Gracie said. 'She was very kind to Cook, her aunt. And she was good to me, mostly.'

'She didn't deserve what happened to her,' I agreed.

Gracie sank back into her bed. I did likewise. There was plenty to ponder. As I drifted off to sleep, I wondered about the family and their connections to Ellen.

★   ★   ★

My bones were stiff by the time we reached the market town. I struggled down from the wagon and helped Mrs Smith down too. She made an arrangement with the driver for when she wanted to be picked up. He touched his forehead politely and went off. We were left rather awkwardly together in the town square.

It was a large, bustling town. The square and the streets leading off it were cobbled and lined with shops. Many had brightly coloured awnings. There were horses and a couple of carriages moving on the streets. Mostly, there were people walking and shopping. Street vendors shouted their wares.

'I hope you enjoy visiting your aunt,' Mrs Smith said kindly.

I'd forgotten my imaginary aunt. 'Thank you, yes I will. I hope you enjoy your afternoon too.'

A sudden crease of her brows suggested otherwise. Then she straightened her back, stamped her umbrella on the ground and made ready to go. 'We can meet here for the driver, Hannah. Don't be late.'

I let her go and pretended to head in the other direction. From a corner of the street, I watched. She walked quickly and deliberately. She had a destination in mind; she wasn't simply wandering around the shops. I'd have to move smartly or I'd lose her.

I wasn't used to playing detective. I tried to imagine Mr Sankey doing this and laughed. He'd be hard pressed to hide his bulky body while following someone. Could I do any better? It wasn't easy. If Mrs Smith glanced back, she'd see me. My main worry was that she'd use more transport. How, then, would I follow?

My fears turned out to be groundless. She kept walking. I ducked into shadows and waited by shop windows as necessary. But she didn't turn around. She marched with purpose out to the edge of the town. Now there were fields. Where was she going?

It was much harder to stay out of sight along the country lanes. Luckily the hedgerows were high and thick. But at this season, there were few leaves left. So I kept a good distance between us.

Around a gentle curve, there appeared a large square building. High walls surrounded it, and I could only make out its upper storey and roof. But I knew what it was. I waited behind the trunk of a tree. Mrs Smith now did indeed glance back. I was hidden from her sight.

The tall gates opened slightly and she was admitted. I stood there, thinking. At least part of the mystery was explained. Mrs Smith was visiting someone in prison. Although she'd told Mrs Pearson she had no family, there was the possibility she'd lied. After all, it was doubtful the Dawtons would want to employ as housekeeper a woman who had a relative in prison.

What if Ellen had followed her? The more I considered that, the more I was convinced I was right. The mystery of where Mrs Smith went on her days off would have been a lure to a girl like Ellen who had to know everything. Maybe she'd hidden behind this very tree, watching, just as I did.

The difference was, I'd never say or do anything to harm Mrs Smith. But what had Ellen done? Had she used this information against the housekeeper? I rather thought so. In which case, what might Mrs Smith have done to shut Ellen up?

I shivered in the freezing air. But it wasn't the temperature that made the goose bumps rise on my skin. I was suddenly afraid. I wished I'd never followed her. What on earth was I playing at?

I pushed against the tree trunk and stepped back. And stifled a scream. A person loomed at me, too close for comfort. I staggered. 'Who are you?' I cried.

'I could ask the same thing.' The old woman gave a gap-toothed grin. She wore a dirty bonnet with greasy ribbons dangling under her chin. Her shawl was holey and her skirts an indecisive colour. She smelt of age and sourness.

'Excuse me,' I muttered, trying to pass.

But she blocked my path. 'Not so fast, dearie. Maybe I can help you.'

'I don't think so. I don't need any help. Let me past, please.'

She leaned towards me and I caught a whiff of her breath. 'Who you watching?'

'No one,' I lied.

She tapped the side of her nose with a grimy finger. 'Secrets aplenty in this part of town. I'm always hungry. Have you a coin or two to spare an old lady?'

Instinctively, my fingers flew to my pocket and my money. Her rheumy eyes followed the movement. Her smile was horrid.

'See, it's like this,' she said conversationally, sidling closer while I held my breath against the stink. 'I know the folks what come around here. You want to know who that woman is? I'll tell you. For a price.'

'I know who that woman is.' I held the back of my hand to my mouth, trying not to breathe in.

She cackled like an old witch. 'If you know that, then you know who's she's visiting. My brother works in there. Has worked there for twenty odd years. Knows the inmates. Knows their little ways. Who gets visitors and who don't. But that don't interest you.' She moved away and waited.

'You say your brother works in the prison?' I had to be certain. I didn't have money to throw away on useless tattle.

She nodded, 'He knows all that goes on in there. If he doesn't know it, it ain't worth knowing. And he tells me it all. He likes a good gossip, does Jimmy.'

I pulled out some coins. She grabbed for them greedily. I held them aloft.

'Who does she visit?' I asked.

'It's her brother. He's in there for stealing and hitting a copper over the head. Won't get out anytime soon either.'

I was horrified. Poor Mrs Smith. To be related to such a bad, monstrous man. But her secret was safe with me. I felt nothing but sympathy for her. I paid the old woman and she shuffled away. The question was, was Mrs Smith capable of killing Ellen? I didn't like to think so. But who could say what might happen in anger and how a scuffle might end?

I was in a sombre mood as I returned to the market town. I looked at the clock tower. There were hours to fill before Mrs Smith and the wagon both returned. I walked about the town, peering into windows at the wares within. I found a haberdashery and purchased a small length of blue ribbon. A woman with a basket of fruit approached. I bought a bag of ripe purple plums. These I'd share with Gracie and Bill.

I idled my time away until I saw the wagon arriving. The driver was rosy-cheeked and friendly. I'd no doubt he'd been in an alehouse or two. The horse seemed to be in charge, stopping the wagon in just the right place. It snorted and then chomped at the weeds sprouting amongst the cobbles.

I climbed up and sat in the wagon. The driver dozed. I was beginning to feel anxious when I saw Mrs Smith's upright person hurrying towards us.

She looked unhappy but managed a smile to greet me.

'I'm sorry to be late,' she said as she took her seat. 'It's most unlike me but was outwith my control.'

The driver hid a belch. That was his only answer. He made noises to the horse and we were off.

'How is your aunt?' Mrs Smith asked me.

'Oh . . . she is very well, thank you.' I was becoming a proficient liar. Feeling ashamed for deceiving her, in turn I asked if she had enjoyed her afternoon. For what else could I do? I didn't wish to upset her, but her face fell before she managed to hide her emotions.

'It was very profitable,' she said with a brief nod.

I searched for further conversation and, finding none, offered her a plum. She was extraordinarily pleased by this.

'Thank you, Hannah. What wonderful plums — such a rich colour. And so tasty. It quite cheers one up.'

I didn't mention her slip of the

tongue. She needed cheering up. An innocent bystander might ask why on such a clear, frosty and perfect day. But I imagined the grim interior of the prison and how its inmates must be, and wished it was otherwise for her.

'What a coincidence, your aunt living in the town,' she said, carefully wiping her fingers with a white handkerchief to remove the sticky plum juice. 'You will no doubt visit her again.'

That was a tricky one. I had no need to come back here. I had the truth of the matter. In fact, I never wanted to see that prison again, or meet the horrible old woman whose brother worked there. So I dissembled.

'I won't be back for a while. My aunt doesn't like visitors too often. She likes to keep herself to herself.'

'But she must have been pleased to see you?'

'Yes, yes, she was. Only I won't go again for some weeks. In fact, I was hoping I might ask you if I could go home soon.'

Now she frowned openly. I squirmed on my hard seat. My fingers were crossed. I longed to see Mam and Dad and Kitty. It was a long journey and I'd need a couple of days away. It was a long shot.

'You are asking quite a favour,' she said. 'It's whether we can manage without you for two days. Still, you've worked hard since you arrived. Leave it with me. I'll let you know.'

I had to be content with that. I hoped she'd say yes. I wasn't homesick exactly. I loved being at Muirfield, despite the murky goings-on. But it'd be nice to see my family.

Soon we were dropped off at the entrance to the estate. The driver mumbled sleepily and waved the horse on. Mrs Smith shook her head at his behaviour.

'I wonder he'll get home. He'll probably end up in a hedge and the horse will go home.'

We both laughed, sharing the joke. Then she looked serious.

'Now it's back to work. We've shared an outing today, and I have to admit I liked having your company. I was feeling a little sorry for myself. None of your business why, but . . . well, it was nice not to be alone. But now, remember your place. I'm the housekeeper and you're the maid. That being so, I will go up the driveway first and you may wait here. Give me five minutes before you start up. Do we understand each other?'

'Yes, Mrs Smith,' I said. We understood each other perfectly.

She smiled at me warmly, then began her walk back up to Muirfield Hall.

9

A Visit Home

A couple of weeks later, I was granted leave to go home. I was so excited I hardly slept. When I woke early, my thoughts turned to Adam. After the gift of the flower at the summerhouse, we'd met but in passing. I continued to take the gardeners their lunch. Adam was rarely about unless I sought him out. He'd be clearing out the greenhouses or pruning one of Muirfield's high hedges. There were many jobs to be done before the winter, he explained.

I was pleased to watch him work, careful not to overstay my welcome. Mrs Pearson had a loud shout and short tether. I didn't want to be banned from taking lunch to the bothy. So it was snippets of delight to be with him. I longed for a day together.

'Wouldn't you like that too?' I asked him.

He shrugged, concentrating on dead-heading some plants withering in pots. 'There's such a lot to do in the garden, I can't be away from it.'

'You can't stay here forever.' I forced a laugh. 'What about us?'

'Us?' He sounded strange.

'Yes, us,' I repeated uncertainly. 'We're . . . you gave me the flower . . . '

He grunted.

Encouraged, I went on, 'We're together, aren't we?'

He didn't deny it.

'So all I want is for us to go somewhere, away from Muirfield.' I named the market town as a possibility.

'Not there. I don't like crowds.' He shook his head.

'Where, then?'

He put down the pot with the unfortunate sick plant. 'I don't know. What's wrong with here?'

'Because we're never on our own,' I said, taking a handful of the soil from

159

the work bench and crumbling it to dust. 'I'd like us to go to a tea room or take in a show.'

'No shows around here.' His lip curled in amusement.

'Oh, you're impossible!' I flung down the dirt and stomped off.

When he didn't follow or shout for me to stay, I came back the next day. I gave Pete the lunch basket and asked for Adam. The old man threw me a kindly look. Adam was in the walled garden and didn't want to be disturbed.

We'll see about that, I thought, heading straight there. I was ready for an argument. I was impatient to move our relationship forward. He hadn't even kissed me yet. I wanted a spring wedding. Between then and now, I needed to get to know him better. My heart was set on all this. It never occurred to me that Adam was dragging his feet. If anything, his slow ways were endearing.

He had his back to me as I went in to the walled garden. I called his name.

He turned, not looking too excited to see me. He had the glazed expression I had come to know only too well. He was thinking about plants. He lived and breathed them. I sighed. I wouldn't complain. Mr Dawton knew his worth. Adam had a good job here. Nothing must jeopardise that, even if I took second place to the shrubs.

'I'm busy,' he said.

'I know. I won't disturb you. I've left your lunch with Pete.'

'Well?'

'I just want to know if you do like me.' There, it was out. All my insecurities.

'I like you.'

'Then prove it,' I said boldly. 'Kiss me.'

He hesitated. I took the twigs from his hand and threw them down. Stroppily, I stood there, hands on hips, defying him not to act. He slowly pulled me to him. I didn't breathe. Then his lips were on mine. They were warm and dry. He pressed my mouth for a second, then drew away. Disappointed, I opened my eyes.

'We must be careful of your reputation,' he said.

There was no one to see us, but I understood. He was protecting me. I sighed. 'Can we go out together?'

His shoulders tensed. Then he nodded. 'You know there's a servants' day out coming up. It happens every year. Mr and Mrs Dawton pay for us to go to the seaside. We'll be together then.'

'It's a bit cold for the seaside,' I said.

'Cheaper out of season. And it's got to be soon, because they're going away to the city for a few weeks. While they're gone, we'll get our day out.'

It was a long speech for Adam. I sensed he wanted rid of me. Well, I was happy to go. I'd got what I wanted. A whole day with him. It was going to be wonderful.

In the meantime, Mrs Smith called me to one side and told me I could start my journey home. 'We've a bit of a lull. You can go for a couple of days, but you must be back to help with the packing. The family are going to Glasgow and taking half the house, if you ask me.'

I was very pleased. I nearly hugged her. She smiled at my delight. 'Now, off with you. There's dusting to be done upstairs.'

* * *

The journey home was long and tiring. I took the wagon as far as the county line. Then I hitched a lift on a farm cart going my way. I had to walk a stretch too. Finally, I made it after a long day and after darkness had fallen. I wasn't afraid. The fields and the soft hooting of owls were familiar. I knocked on the cottage door and pushed it open.

Three faces stared at me. A few candles flickered, casting yellow light. The fire burned and glowed. 'It's our Hannah,' Kitty cried, coming to greet me.

I had to brush away a tear as I hugged them. It was hard working so far from home.

'Come away in,' Mam said, herding me to the table.

Dad sat with a big grin on his face. 'My lass, my bonny lass. Is it really you?'

'It's me, Dad. It really is.'

His eyes were wet too as we embraced again. He held me as if he'd never let me go. Gently, I pulled away and sat next to him. Mam pushed a plate of vegetable soup at me. They all watched as I gulped it down. I'd not eaten all day apart from breakfast at Muirfield. She poured a cup of tea, brown as peat water, and set it down. It was hot but I drank it fast. Then, feeling much better, I picked up my bag. 'Cook has sent some presents for you.'

'We don't need charity,' Mam said swiftly.

'It's not charity, it's a kindness, that's all. Here, open that.' I passed her a wrapped lump.

Mrs Pearson had put in cheese from the estate, some root vegetables, a pot of blackberry jam and a large pound cake.

'Cut that up, lass,' Dad said to Kitty, pointing to the cake. 'We'll have a slice each with the jam.'

'We should keep it,' Mam said. 'We've eaten enough today.'

But Dad would have none of it. He waved her away. 'It's a celebration. Hannah's home. Come on and taste this cake. It's delicious.'

Mam allowed us to bully her into eating a thick slab of it slathered with the dark, sweet jam. She didn't comment but finished it all. Dad's breathing was laboured. She ordered him back to bed. He didn't argue, and I promised to come in soon and sit with him.

'How is he?' I asked her.

'He's no worse and he's no better. Which makes it all the more important you keep that job and don't get laid off.'

'I'm well settled in there, and there's plenty of work. I'm not worried.'

She sniffed. 'It's nice to see you, lass.'

'And you, Mam.'

'Why did they let you come home?' She picked up the remaining cake crumbs and licked her fingers.

'Because they're good people. Mrs Smith is the housekeeper and a very fair boss. Mrs Pearson is the cook and a lovely, generous woman. I didn't ask for this food to be sent; she made it all up for me to take.'

And I told them all about Muirfield, describing the people and the place as best I was able. Mam and Kitty hung on every word. Later, I sat with Dad and repeated some of my tales. He got tired quickly and fell asleep. I tucked up his covers to keep him warm and tiptoed out.

It was late. Mam had gone to bed. The fire still burned, and Kitty added another peat sod. I wasn't tired. It was cosy in the darkness with only the firelight and two dripping candles. The smells of peat and wax were so homely.

'Tell me all your news,' Kitty said, settling back in her seat.

'I told you all about the house and the people already. There's nothing more to tell.'

'Ah, but there is. You've met someone, haven't you?' Kitty clapped her hands together.

'How did you know?'

'You're my sister. I know you like I know myself. Now spit it out.'

'I'm getting married,' I said, and was properly pleased when she hugged me.

'Who's the lucky man?'

'His name is Adam. He's one of the gardeners at Muirfield. Actually, he's the best gardener. He's ambitious. One day he's going to be head gardener there or he'll move somewhere bigger. *We'll* move. We'll have a maid to tend us and our own house.' I was getting carried away.

'And you love him? You are in love with him?' Kitty asked.

'Do you need to ask me that? He's

the handsomest man this side of the country.'

'As Mam says, handsome is as handsome does. Is he kind to you? Is he generous and loving?'

I paused. They weren't the first qualities that sprang to mind about Adam. But I brushed that aside. He was perfect and he had chosen me. I was going to be Mrs Adam Fairlow. And nothing my sister Kitty said was going to dissuade me. She didn't know Adam. She wasn't in a position to judge him.

'Yes, he's all that,' I said, not wanting an argument on my first night home.

'Then that's all you need,' Kitty said sagely, older than her years.

'Och, what do you know,' I said rudely.

We both grinned. Her teeth gleamed in the firelight. The grins turned to giggles. This was what I'd missed about home. The good times Kitty and I had shared growing up.

'When's the wedding?'

'I want a spring wedding. Winter's so

dull and horrible. It'll be nice to get married when the flowers are out.' Adam would like that.

'Where will you live?'

'I believe we'll get a cottage on the estate. Mr Dawton thinks the world of Adam, so I reckon we'll get a nice big roomy place.'

'And a maid to tend you,' Kitty teased.

I blushed. 'Well, maybe not immediately. But one day, when Adam's in charge, then yes. I'll be mistress of my own home.'

It wasn't so long ago that I'd had no ambitions in life other than to have a job. Now listen to me. I'd plans as long as my legs. It was lovely to share them with Kitty.

'I heard a few choice stories about Muirfield,' she said casually.

'What do you mean?'

'You know Brigid O'Connell?'

'Yes, Brigid who told you about the place at the Hall. Brigid who brings the washing.'

'That Brigid, the very one. Well, she knows a lass called Agnes Tiller who lives two villages over, and Agnes has a cousin who lives in Muirfield village. And Agnes's cousin, James, has a pal who works for a man who sells a bit of this and that.'

'Where are you going with this? I'm thoroughly confused.'

'What I heard from Brigid is that the butler at Muirfield has a nice little earner going on.'

'Mr Joseph?' I was shocked. I'd thought it a few bottles of wine he was snaffling. But this was bigger.

Kitty nodded, satisfied with my reaction. She leaned further back in her seat to catch the fire's warmth. The glow caught the copper tints in her hair and lit them up. 'Apparently he sells on food and wines from the Hall. Not in huge amounts, but a goodly trickle. James's pal has seen it all.'

I could hardly believe it. Mr Joseph gave every impression of being principled and above everyone else. To think he was nothing but a common thief! If Ellen had found out, then she'd more than a few bottles of wine in a hold over him. Then I had a thought.

'If James and his pal and Agnes and Brigid and now you and I know about this, it's not much of a secret, is it?'

'But who's going to tell on him? If you tried when you get back, are they going to take your word as a maid over his word as the butler? I don't think so. You and me, Brigid and Agnes and the others, we're not important. No one's going to listen to us. Your Mr Joseph is in no danger.'

If that was true, then did Ellen have a sway over him at all?

'What is it now?' Kitty asked. 'Your face is all scrunched up, like when you're thinking and getting nowhere.'

I told her about Ellen and my suspicions and concerns. 'It seems to me that Ellen had more power than us. If what you say is right, she was blackmailing people or at least threatening them with what she knew. Mr

Joseph's crimes passed along to Mr Dawton by, say the housekeeper, would work. Even if the housekeeper didn't want to tell, she might have to, to prevent her own secrets coming out.'

'What a tangled web.' I yawned.

'You never told Mam and Dad you were getting married.'

'I forgot. I'll tell them tomorrow. Right now, I need my sleep.'

We banked up the fire and took a candle each to light our way. I snuggled in next to Kitty and the years fell away. It was good to be home.

* * *

We were up with the dawn. The cockerel screeched his morning welcome to the world. I helped Ma make porridge and set out four bowls, hot and steaming. I roused Dad from his slumber. 'Breakfast's ready.'

'The sight of your face is food enough for me.'

'I wish I could stay,' I said, 'but I

must get back today.' I helped him sit up and offered to bring the porridge to him. It was a sign of his health that he agreed. We ate together in companionable silence. Then, empty bowls in hand, I left him to get ready.

'Must you go so soon?' he said.

'I'm sorry, but yes. I'll walk over to the crossroads; the farmer's going to pick me up on his way. I mustn't miss him. Mrs Smith needs me back. There's always work to be done.' I made sure to sound bright and cheerful while inside my heart was breaking. For when would I see him again?

I told Mam about my wedding plans at the kitchen table. She and Kitty had left their porridge to cool and now tucked in. I took the heavy kettle from the fire and poured tea for all of us. I sat, savouring the moment, tucking the memories deep into my head, to be taken out and mulled over in my attic bed at Muirfield. They were chatting about the next bundles of sewing and washing to be done.

'You want to stay this morning and scrub a few blouses?' Kitty teased.

'Only if you come back with me and dust a storey of the Hall and peel a mountain of carrots,' I said.

'I wish I could.'

There was envy in her voice. I'd forgotten that what to me was simply work, to Kitty was a strange and desirable activity. She was forever stuck at home because of her leg.

'It's not as much fun as it sounds,' I said. 'I'd much rather be here than there.'

There was a long pause. Then Mam rapped her knuckles on the wood. 'Kitty says there's something you have to say to me.'

'I'm getting married.'

Mam's jaw dropped. 'You never mentioned it last night.'

'I forgot. I was so pleased to see you all.'

'It's a big thing to forget, all the same.' She stared at me carefully. 'Who's the fellow?'

'His name is Adam,' I said, letting his

dear name roll off my tongue, for the joy of saying it. 'He's the gardener at Muirfield.'

'They've just the one, for such a large place?' Mam was quick off the mark. Too shrewd.

'No, there's Mr Crickett — he's the head gardener — and there's Pete; but Adam's got the most talent.'

Kitty and Mam shared a glance. They didn't quite roll their eyes, but I saw Mam's mouth quirk like she wanted to laugh. I was boasting about my man. It was true. I couldn't help it.

'Dad and I want to meet him.'

I hadn't thought of that. As I was barely able to get Adam to leave the garden for the village teashop, what chance had I of getting him to undertake the journey here?

'And you'll get married from our church in the village.' This was said firmly, allowing no room for argument.

'I'll ask him.'

'You won't ask him, you'll tell him. It's traditional for the wedding to be from the bride's home. Besides, Dad can't travel far.'

That put an end to any discussion. Mam was right — Dad was too poorly to go any distance. And I wanted him to see me wed.

'You'll marry in the church and have a meal here, right and proper.' Mam sighed but it was a good sigh, not her usual sad one. More a satisfaction and anticipation of what was to come.

They waved me off as I stepped out towards the crossroads. My load was lighter as I had no food and gifts to carry. I had but a slice of bread and cheese for my meal. My emotions were mixed. I was eager to get back to Muirfield and to Adam and my friends Gracie and Bill. Yet underneath, there was a current of unease, like darker, more treacherous currents in an otherwise peaceful river. Someone or something was waiting for me there. I felt it in my belly.

10

Night-time Shadows

The house was in an uproar. Mrs Smith was right; the family's visit to Glasgow meant a lot of packing boxes. They were to be away for a month. Mrs Dawton was the happiest I've ever seen her. She flitted from room to room, barking orders. Mrs Smith was quite harassed. She managed to keep her dignity while following her mistress and writing notes. Certain items must be taken. Others were dismissed, only to be snatched up once more. Perhaps Mrs Dawton would take her painting easel after all. Miss Alice must have her violin to practise. On second thoughts, put it back, there's a violin in Glasgow she can use. And so it went on.

They had no house of their own in the city and were to stay with friends.

Mrs Dawton was going to use the holiday to search for a townhouse. Whilst her spirits were high, Mr Dawton's were considerably lower. Any glimpse of the master showed a bowed figure with drooping features. He couldn't bear to be away from his beloved gardens.

It turned out that Miss Emily was not going. According to Mrs Dawton, the child was poorly and so must remain at Muirfield. She was to be cared for by her governess, and Mrs Smith was to oversee the rest. I didn't think Emily was ill; rather that her sleep was more and more disturbed by nightmares and night walking. I imagined it was an embarrassment to her mother, and not behaviour likely to sit well amongst their Glasgow hosts.

'The master has left a long list of instructions,' Adam grumbled when I sneaked out to see him. 'As if I don't know what I'm about. I don't need him telling me.'

'He is the owner of the gardens,' I

said, thinking this a bit much.

'He's a fool,' Adam muttered. 'He doesn't know the half of what he's got in here. Little tender plants I've brought on, he doesn't have a clue about. He likes the showy blossoms, the unusual colours, but he's missing what's important.'

I didn't understand him, but, bored with plants, I didn't ask further. 'My mam and dad want to meet you.'

'This is going too fast.' He kicked at a set of pots and one fell, chipping its rim.

I held my breath. What did he mean? 'You still like me?' I whispered.

'I like you, Hannah, but let's take this slowly. The best plants grow from small shoots.' His fingers curled on mine, and their warmth and strength thrilled me.

'All right,' I agreed. 'I'm sorry. I shouldn't have pushed for getting wed so soon. Or for you to meet my family.'

He nodded and let my fingers go. I waited, but he hadn't more to say. I was deeply disappointed. It seemed wrong to me. If we liked each other and were walking out, then marriage was the only solution, at least for a respectable girl like me. Why wait? Spring was far enough away. I decided not to nag on it. I'd raise the subject gently soon.

Miss Emily was unsettled by all the chaos. She wandered the house, pale and wan. Cook was at her wits' end as the girl inevitably was drawn to the warm comfort of the kitchen.

'I'm forever tripping over her,' Mrs Pearson grumbled.

'She doesn't like all the noise. She had her hands over her ears when I came in,' I said.

'Poor mite. I must be more charitable.' Cook sighed. 'In fact, I'll make some of her favourite ginger biscuits. That'll cheer her up.'

Despite her occasional shouting, Mrs Pearson had a heart of gold. 'Did Ellen like your ginger biscuits?' I asked.

Her eyes widened. 'What a funny thing to ask. What made you think on my dear niece?'

Ellen was never off my mind. But I could hardly say that to her aunt. 'I don't know. She was lucky to have you as her aunt. Must've been nice to have a close relative working in the same house.'

'It was very nice,' Cook agreed. 'She came down to the kitchen such a lot. Interested in everything, she was. Such a curious, bright sort of girl. It's hard that she's gone.'

I'll bet she was interested and curious. No doubt she was gathering fuel for her wicked power games. She came to the kitchen where she could spy on Mr Joseph and Mrs Smith and pick up gossip on all the people in the Hall.

But now Cook was speaking again. 'Is it true that you and Adam are courting?'

'We are,' I said cautiously. Partly this was because I wasn't sure myself anymore what was between me and Adam. He was reluctant to commit but yet he liked me. Was my love for him driving all before me? I reminded myself that he hadn't said no to us getting wed. Therefore he must love me. I was cautious too, in that Ellen had been involved with him. I didn't want to upset Mrs Pearson.

She shook her head. 'Well, Hannah, I've become fond of you. You're a hard worker and don't complain. So I'll give you a piece of advice — the same advice I gave Ellen. Take care.'

'I don't understand.'

'He's not the marrying kind.'

'But he and Ellen were going to be wed? I thought that was so.' Hadn't Gracie said that? I tried to remember. She'd said they were lovebirds; that although it had cooled a little, it was bound to end in a wedding. I wondered then why things had cooled between them.

Mrs Pearson set out the ingredients for the ginger biscuits. Her hands must always be busy, even when she was conversing. Mixing bowls, wooden spoon, flour and sugar. Sweet-smelling ginger spice and a block of fresh butter.

'He asked her to marry him, that's true. Ellen told me herself. So happy, she was. I've never seen her smiling so much. But why, then, was there no preparation for the marriage? A girl must get her bottom drawer ready. I saw no sign of sewing or laying down of goods. He never came to talk to me about it. And I was her only living relative. It was downright odd.'

'Did you ask Ellen about it?'

The cook scratched her head through her cap. 'I did. I never got a straight answer. She was confident it would all work out. And look how things did turn out. My darling girl, gone forever.'

I felt a shiver, a sudden chill despite the warm cheeriness of the kitchen. Instead of a wedding, there had been a funeral in Ellen's future.

★ ★ ★

I found myself thinking about it a few nights later. The Dawtons were to set off early the next morning. Everything was packed and ready. There was an air of anticipation amongst the servants. Without the family in residence, it was going to be easier, with lighter workloads. We might even get an extra afternoon off. Besides, the day out to the seaside was coming up. I couldn't wait.

I was surprised to feel utterly awake. I stared at the attic ceiling. There were black, jutting shadows; and when I turned my head to the window, I saw there was a full, bright white moon like a circle of good cheese. It was the middle of the night. Gracie's snores echoed in the room. Nothing was visible of her except a tuft of hair.

What had gone wrong between Ellen and Adam? It popped into my head and didn't leave. It had woken me up. Things had cooled. But why? I rubbed my eyes, turned my face to the pillow and attempted to sleep. But it refused to come. I was too alert. With a sigh, I sat up and got out of bed. Perhaps I might light the candle and read a little.

Reaching for the candle, I glanced out of the window. The moonlight made the view of the gardens clear. There below, a patch of white floated across my gaze before disappearing into the dark trees. I blinked. What was it? The candle quite forgotten, I pressed my nose to the glass, trying to see more. The black shadowed woods had swallowed any movement. Beyond, there was a glitter of moonlight on the waters of the lake.

Without conscious decision, I picked up my coat and put it on, and laced up my boots. Then, tiptoeing quietly so as not to wake Gracie, I slipped out of the room. Someone dressed in white had walked in the gardens, through the woods towards the summerhouse and lake. Who was it, so late at night?

It was strange to be sneaking through the house in the silent, small hours. My heart was thudding. The ornaments and furniture made odd shapes. I half-expected a figure to leap out and grab me. I pressed down upon my imagination. I was no child to fear the darkness. The house was full of sleeping people, it was safe.

The main entrance to Muirfield was bolted. I knew it would be so. Mr Joseph was very particular about that. However, on checking the kitchen door, I found it to be unlocked. Not only that, it was ajar.

I hesitated only briefly, then pushed it open and stepped outside. I closed it behind me. The night air was cold and sharp and the moonlight made it easy to see. Curiosity pushed me on. I hurried round the corner towards the potting sheds and greenhouses. As I went by the stables, I heard the snickers of the horses, restless at the person passing them. I thought of Adam as I went past the bothy. He was so close. I was half-tempted to wake him to join me, but pride held me back. I wasn't scared, I told myself.

Where the path met the trees it was different. The path was bright while the trees were almost black. I felt a stirring in the air as if I could sense someone had been this way. Had the figure in white gone on to the lake? Or were they in the woods, waiting?

I swallowed twice. A cough welled up but I stifled it. I wanted no noise attending me. If I was lucky, could I walk in silence, calling no attention? I took a step inside the shadow of the trees.

There was a muffled quality to the sounds now. A creaking of ancient boughs. The rasp of feathers as a bird flew. Scurrying noises as some small creature fled amongst the leaf litter. A light wind had got up, making the tops of the trees sway. I was glad of it. It meant I walked with less fear of discovery.

There was no one on the path. I made it through the woods and sighed in relief. Ahead, I saw the shape of the summerhouse and beyond, the murky waters of the lake. The moonlight was so pretty as it glittered there. It was like diamonds scattered on black velvet.

But where was the figure? I hadn't

dreamt it, had I? I began to worry that I'd left the safety of the house for no reason. But as I skirted round the summerhouse, I saw her. Miss Emily, clad in only a white cotton nightgown, sitting cross-legged on the wooden platform and gazing out at the water.

'Emily, what are you doing here?' I asked.

She didn't reply. She didn't even react. Instead, she continued to stare at the lake. I moved beside her and looked more closely. Her eyes were open but strangely glassy. I waved my fingers in front of her face. No response. She wasn't shivering from the cold. She was trance-like. Mrs Pearson's words came back to me. *She doesn't just dream, you see. She sleepwalks.* She was asleep! But what had drawn her to the lake? I followed her glassy stare. There was nothing but sinister-looking water. Even the ducks had abandoned it, no doubt finding shelter from foxes in the grasses.

'What is it, what do you see?' I whispered to her.

She whimpered in her sleep. I gently took her hand. It was ice cold. I took her other hand and warmed them in mine. Should I wake her? Was it even possible? I had no idea. We sat together for a short while. It was oddly peaceful. The summerhouse at our backs sheltered us from the worst of the wind. The water made slapping and sucking sounds as it hit the muddy edges.

'We should go back,' I said eventually.

I didn't know if she heard me or understood. I stood up and took off my coat. With some effort, I managed to put the coat on her. She allowed me to pull her to standing. Then she stood while I buttoned it up. I was only in my night dress now, and it was very chilly.

We moved slowly round the side of the summerhouse. Now the woods were again visible. The lake was to our backs. I decided we'd walk slowly back to the house. With any luck, I'd get Emily upstairs to her bed without disturbing the rest of the household.

Even as this went through my mind, an unpleasant prickling rose up on my skin. I had the oddest sensation of being watched. I clutched the girl's hand tighter. 'Come on, Miss Emily. We need to go.'

She muttered a few words, but they were so low I couldn't make them out. Her fingers curled on mine. I hoped she understood she was safe with me. I struck out towards the trees. There was no other way to go. To reach Muirfield Hall, we had to follow the path from the lake, through the woods, past the cottages and stables and finally the blessed safety of the kitchen door.

I was scared now. Something wasn't right. It was nothing I could pinpoint; just a sixth sense of danger. A primeval part of me had flickered into life. There was nowhere to hide. So we had to go on.

She came with me, slowly plodding until I wanted to scream at her to hurry up. I'd rather we ran together, past any bogey man or sprite. Did I really think someone was there? I didn't know. I had a lively imagination, as Mam had told me often enough growing up. Wasn't that a good part of the reason for my pursuit of the mystery of Ellen Munroe's murder? I liked to know answers. My mind conjured them easily enough. But I preferred to know the truth.

'It's going to be all right,' I said to Emily, pulling her with me.

But we went slowly by the trees. If anything, she was moving slower. The black trunks were like sentries either side of us. We moved on. Now I was certain someone was behind us. I glanced back. There was nothing. Yet underneath our own breathing and the natural sounds of the woods, I heard the snap of twigs and the rustling of dead leaves. A creature, large, moving about, off the path.

I saw, with thanks, the break in the cover that signalled the path onto open ground. Beyond was the gardener's bothy and other buildings. Goodness, I thought with an inward grin, I'd be glad even for the company of the horses.

Something heavy shoved me from behind and I fell onto the ground. I heard running footsteps, and with a groan, I struggled up. Confused, I stared about me. Where was Emily? Then I was aware I wasn't alone. Pete, the gardener, was crouching beside me, looking concerned.

'Did you have a fall? Why are you out here this time of night?'

'Where's Miss Emily?' I gasped.

'She's right here,' he said.

Emily appeared from behind the nearest tree trunk. She was wide-eyed and awake.

'Did you see someone?' I asked Pete.

He shook his head. 'Only you two. Why?'

'It doesn't matter. I'll take Miss Emily back to the house. She's been sleepwalking.'

'Right you are, Hannah,' Pete said. 'I'll walk with you as far as the cottages.'

We walked in silence, the three of us. My palms stung where I had landed hard upon them on the gritty surface of the path. I was convinced that someone had pushed me. Who was it? And was it a warning? Why had Pete not seen anyone? I didn't know the answers to any of these questions.

I was never so glad to see the house. We left Pete at the gardeners' bothy and made for the kitchen entrance ourselves. I took Emily upstairs and waited until she was tucked into her bed. She, at least, was none the worse for the adventure. She'd only a pair of dirty feet to show for it.

I jumped at every shadow as I made for my attic bedroom. I was more afraid than I'd ever been. Someone didn't want people roaming in the night at Muirfield. And I didn't know who that was, or why.

★　★　★

Gracie was awake when I tried to get quietly into bed. I was shivering uncontrollably, from shock or the cold or both. My teeth chattered so loudly that my jaw ached.

'Hannah? Is that you?' she mumbled sleepily.

'Sorry. I didn't mean to wake you up,' I whispered. 'Go back to sleep.'

'Where have you been?' Gracie demanded, looking at once not sleepy at all. She sat up in bed, her hair like a haystack.

'Keep your voice down,' I said. 'We don't want Sarah coming to complain.'

I took off my boots and got into bed. I realised that Emily still had my coat. No matter; I'd retrieve it in the morning when the Dawtons had departed for Glasgow.

'Tell me what's been happening.'

'All right. Give me a moment to get warm.' I rubbed my hands together, then winced at the pain in my palms. They were scraped from my fall. I took the blankets and wrapped them snugly round me. Gradually I felt a little better. The warmth seeped into me and I began to relax. In fact, the whole incident felt like a dream of sorts.

'Hannah?'

So I told her what had happened. She was silent for a while, digesting it all.

'What was Pete doing out there in the woods?'

I stared at her admiringly. She was as sharp as a tack. I hadn't thought to ask that. I put the blame on the shock my fall had given me. I'd have got there eventually. 'I don't know. All I do know is that he was there beside me as I tried to get up.'

'Isn't that a bit suspicious?' Gracie frowned. 'Maybe he's the one who shoved you, then he pretended he'd come to help.'

I thought about the old man. He'd always been very kind to me. I thought of the kind way he cleaned the bothy and laid out the lunches. Of the little posies of flowers that brightened up their table. I couldn't imagine him hurting me.

'How long's he worked here?' I asked Gracie.

'Forever. He's been here all the years I've worked here, and I came at the age of ten.'

'Has he been involved in anything . . . unsavoury before now? Has he a reputation for anger or violence?'

She laughed, then put her fist to her mouth to stop the noise. 'No, I've not heard any gossip to suggest that.'

I relaxed, until she spoke again. 'Still, if he's got something to hide . . . Men will do extreme things to keep their secrets hidden.'

Uneasily, I shifted in my bed. 'He'd have some cheek pushing me over and then pretending he'd found me and asking if I was all right.'

'Who knows what he's capable of — that's the point,' Gracie said, warming to her theme. 'Look at May Litton. We all knew she was a one for the lads, but I'd never have guessed she'd actually run away with one of them. It's ruined her reputation, such as it was. That was a step too far even for May. People do strange things under pressure.'

'Yes, but what if it wasn't old Pete? What if there was someone else there?' I swallowed down my fear. It was a horrible thought, that I'd been stalked like a big cat with its prey. 'I felt like I was being watched. Then when Emily and I were walking along the path, I heard what sounded like footsteps in the forest, crunching on twigs and breaking the leaf litter.'

'Whoever it was, why did they push you?'

'To warn me off.' I was convinced of that.

'But to warn you off what, exactly? Walking in the woods at night?'

'Yes, I think that's it. Whatever they want to hide, it's got to be in the woods.'

'And you think that Ellen found it?' Grade's voice held a trembling excitement.

'You're right. That's got to be it.' Some detective I was. Gracie was so much better at it than me.

'Did Miss Emily see what happened?'

'She didn't say. She was right there when I got up. But she didn't say one word when we walked back to the house, not even after we'd left Pete at the bothy.'

'She was sleepwalking, so she might not remember much.'

'It was quite strange seeing her like that,' I said. 'But I'm sure she was awake when I fell. The question is, did my fall wake her up, or was she already awake when the mysterious person pushed me?'

'I don't believe we are any closer to learning the truth about Ellen,' Gracie said.

'Don't you? Because I do. Someone is rattled. And rattled people make mistakes,' I said firmly.

'I hope you're not suggesting what I think you're suggesting,' Gracie said, sounding horrified.

I nodded. 'Yes, I am. Soon I'm going to take another walk in the woods at night.' I felt slightly sick as I said this. I didn't feel brave at all.

'That's an awful idea. I won't let you.'

Dear Gracie. What a good friend she was. Defending me against my own judgement. 'I won't pretend I like the notion either,' I said, 'but what else is there to do?'

'I'll tell you — leave the detective games for Mr Arthur Sankey, that's what. I've a good mind to tell Mrs Smith what you're up to.'

'You wouldn't!'

'Try me. You're going to get yourself killed if you're not careful. I won't let you.' She was tearful now.

I got out of my bed and ran to hers. I hugged her hard. 'Please don't cry, Gracie.'

'I'll stop if you promise not to go into the woods alone at night.'

'And if I don't?'

'Then I will tell Mrs Smith and she'll make sure you can't do it.'

Gracie was like a tiny, fierce tiger snarling at me. A part of me wanted to laugh at her. Another part was annoyed that she'd thwarted my grand plan. 'I promise.'

She pushed me away. I got back into my bed. We stared at one another. Gracie was the first to speak.

'I want to know who killed Ellen. Especially if he or she is still at Muirfield. But I don't want to lose you. I'm sorry, Hannah, but you do see it's for the best?'

I sighed and lay back, the blankets pulled now to my chin where they tickled me. 'Let's go to sleep. Things might look different in the morning.'

11

A Day at the Seaside

A charabanc had been hired for the servants' day out. There was a buzz of excitement when it arrived, driven by a man in a battered stovepipe hat and pulled by a honey-coloured horse.

There were fifteen of us to be carried in it to the seaside. A caretaker from the village was to stay behind for security. Miss Emily and her governess were not joining us, of course. But from the staff, even the young stable hands were coming. There was a festive feel to the atmosphere as we climbed up and took our places. I sat between Gracie and Janet. In the row ahead were Mrs Smith and Mrs Pearson. Behind us were Sarah, Bill and one of the lads from the stables. I looked anxiously for Adam. He was the last to arrive. I tried to catch his eye, but he was busy finding a place at the back to sit so I gave up. I'd have all day with him when we got there. The journey was only an hour along a reasonable road to the coast.

'It's a pity the day out isn't in the summer,' I remarked.

Gracie nudged me in the ribs. 'Well, if that was the case, you'd have missed it altogether.'

'That's so,' I agreed with a laugh. 'Still, we won't be paddling or bathing today.'

'I don't think Mrs Smith would let us do that even in the summer.'

'She can't be everywhere at once,' I said cheekily.

Gracie laughed too. Even Janet managed a weak, toothy grin. The usual hierarchy was loosened. I heard Mr Joseph chatting to the driver, and the housekeeper and Cook had their heads together for a gossip. Behind us, Sarah was attempting to get Bill to talk. He wasn't saying much, from what I managed to overhear. It didn't put her off. She flirted with him and asked if he liked her new bonnet. I hoped Bill wasn't going to make the mistake of going back to her. She wasn't good enough for him.

My first view of the sea was breath-taking. The charabanc stopped on a rise and we all sighed and pointed. Despite the lateness of the season, the day was bright and warm. The sea was invitingly blue, and the sky had only patchy cloud cover. I prayed it'd stay nice. I wanted so very much to enjoy the day. I pictured me and Adam arm in arm walking across the beach.

The charabanc rumbled down the slope of the road and into the seaside village. The driver parked it near the promenade, where there was a patch of grass for the horse to crop. The men descended from the vehicle and offered help to the women. It was a bit of a step to get down, especially in long skirts. There was an awkward moment when it was my turn. I paused, waiting for Adam to step forward and guide me.

Instead he chose that moment to turn his back to our crowd and stare out at the sea. The colour rose in my cheeks. Bill stepped forward and gave me his hand. Sarah glared at me. Gladly, I let Bill help me down. He smiled.

'I hope you enjoy your day out. You know, there's a very nice teashop on the seafront.'

'Perhaps we'll all meet there later for tea and cake,' I said with a smile. 'But first, I want to touch the sand. It looks so lovely.'

He grinned at my enthusiasm. 'I'll come with you. It's ages since I've been here. In fact, it was last year's outing.'

Sarah cut in front of us with a sweet, icy smile. 'Bill, I'd like to visit the shops. Will you accompany me? It won't do to go alone, Mrs Smith won't allow it.'

'Of course,' he said politely. Then to me, in an aside with a wink, 'We'll catch up later on the beach. Save me a seashell or two.'

Sarah hooked her arm quite firmly in

his and walked away. She threw me a look over her shoulder. It spoke of triumph. Poor Bill — I hoped he knew what he was in for. She was clearly determined to win him back. He was such a nice fellow.

Before long, Bill and Sarah faded from my worries. I searched for Adam. Mr Joseph was giving orders, waving his large pocket watch at the group.

'We will return to the charabanc at four o'clock precisely. Do not be late. If you are in any doubt, there is a church tower with a clock in the village square. Enjoy yourselves, but do remember that we represent the Dawton family at all times. There must be no unseemly behaviour.'

He'd hardly finished speaking before everyone dispersed. Bill and Sarah had edged away to the echo of his last words. The young lads were on the steps from the promenade to the sands. With a whoop, one of them jumped down. Mr Joseph didn't hear. He was busy escorting Mrs Smith and Mrs

Pearson to the nearest teashop, where I imagined they'd spend the hours until we went home. Gracie decided she'd go with Janet to look at what was for sale. She promised to find me later in the teashop.

'Adam,' I said as I linked my arm with his, the way Sarah had with Bill, 'shall we walk along the beach?'

'If you will,' he said.

'What do you want to do? I'm happy to come with you.'

'There's not much to do. It's a dreadful waste of a day.'

'Why did you come then?' I cried, annoyed at his attitude. His love of Muirfield and its precious gardens was irksome.

He shrugged. 'No choice. Mr Joseph insists all the staff attend. It's stupid when I've got so much work to do.'

'Not so much that you can't enjoy a day out to the seaside, surely?'

He fixed me with his blue stare. Even though he was clearly annoyed, I was drawn, as ever, to the beauty of him.

'Every day, every minute that I breathe,

is a determination to better myself. I'm not bound to be at Muirfield forever. In fact, I'm not going to be there beyond a year. I've got plans, big plans, and I'm bent on carrying them through. And nobody, *nobody* is getting in the way of that. Do you hear?'

I took an involuntary step back. The vehemence in his voice was somehow shocking. His face was fierce with passion — a passion not directed at me but rather at his work, his beloved plants.

I think, in that fleeting moment, that something shifted inside me. A shift in my belief in him. And in my hopes for the future. But I didn't realise it right there. I was only upset with him snarling at me.

'Is this why your courtship with Ellen faded?' I blurted out.

He looked surprised. 'What?'

'Gracie told me you were like lovebirds but then it cooled between you,' I said.

He made a noise deep down in his throat in disgust. 'You women, is it all you talk about? Love and marriage. Is there nothing better to discuss?'

'It's what life is about, isn't it? It's the basis for happiness and security.'

'You're wrong. The basis for happiness and security is money. And I intend to make a lot.'

'Did Ellen get in the way of your plans? Is that it?'

His expression shut down. 'I'm going back to the charabanc.'

I watched him go. His shoulders were stiff with anger, and his gait too. What had just happened? My eyes pooled with tears. Barely able to see, I turned away and stumbled down onto the beach. I was not going to let our argument spoil my day. It was hard not to think about it. I crouched down and picked up a handful of sand. It was cold, damp and gritty. I raised it to my nose. The smell of briny sea and cockles cheered me. I sprinkled it slowly back onto the beach. Feeling marginally happier, I decided to walk out to the tide line.

The sea was far out. The waves

rushed in on a friendly roar and were sucked back out. The gleaming wet sand was smooth like caramel. I trod on it. My footsteps too were smoothed away. There were gulls crying overhead. I saw the stable hands further along the strand. They were shouting to each other and throwing pebbles into the surf. An immense peace settled upon me. I drew the fresh air into my lungs.

I'd walk along the beach, I decided. There was a bluff about a mile away. The exercise would do me good and blow away my demons.

I set off at a good pace. There were not many people on the beach; it was too late in the season for it to be busy. Two women with umbrellas and a small dog passed me. They were well dressed and probably local gentry. I liked their pretty bonnets. The small dog's tongue lolled and made it look as if he was smiling.

My spirits rose. I'd not think upon Adam. Was he really brooding in the charabanc? Now that was a waste of the day. We were not likely to get another day at the seaside for many months. I thought how nice to would be to visit in the spring or summer.

As I wandered along, I saw many pink and white shells. I picked a few that were not broken or chipped. Their surfaces were silky to the touch. They too smelt of the sea. I was beginning to feel quite hungry. The good sea air was working its magic.

I heard my name called. There was Bill, waving and heading towards me. No sign of Sarah.

'Hello. I thought it was you. You're striding out very determined.' His face was flushed with the fresh air and his brown eyes sparkled.

'I'm walking until the bluff.' I indicated the blocky outcrop beyond. 'Will you join me?'

He set his stride to match mine.

'Wait a minute,' I said, and delved into my pockets. 'Here.' I pulled out the shells and gave them to him.

'What beauties.' Bill smiled enthusiastically. 'Do you want them back?'

'They're for you.' I half did want to keep them. They'd look nice on my cabinet in the bedroom. But it was worth it for Bill's genuine eagerness. He slipped them into his pocket.

'Where's Sarah?' I asked casually.

'She didn't want to get her boots dirty on the sand. She went to the teashop instead. I said we'd meet her there.'

'But not before we finish our beach walk?' I didn't want to spend any more time with Sarah than was strictly necessary. I was certain she felt the same way about me.

'Of course. Look out there. Is that a seal?'

I looked where his finger pointed. It was indeed — a large, round and friendly-looking face bobbed up out of the sea, not too far away. I saw two liquid black eyes gazing at us curiously. I held my breath. How wonderful. I'd never seen one except in the pictures of a book.

'It *is* a seal, I'm sure,' I whispered, not wanting to frighten the animal away. 'Or is it a mermaid?'

'No hair, so it can't be a mermaid,' Bill commented.

I giggled. The fresh air was getting to me. I hadn't felt this relaxed and happy for a long while. The atmosphere at Muirfield was tense and thick, I suddenly realised. The shadow of Ellen's death was pervasive. It didn't help that Arthur Sankey haunted the house. He was a reminder of all that was wrong there. But it took coming here to the seaside to make me see all that.

'Is everything all right?' Bill asked.

I glanced at him. 'Is it obvious? Adam and I had an argument. He's gone to sit in the charabanc.'

Bill looked tactfully away from me. The seal dived under the water. The sea's surface was at once mysterious. Anything could lurk and move and swim underneath and we wouldn't know about it.

'Are you sure about marrying Adam?' he said at last.

'Of course!' Annoyance flared.

He put up both palms as if to ward

me off. 'I do apologise. It's none of my business.'

We walked in an awkward silence for a few minutes, nothing but the sounds of the sea and the birds and our feet crunching on the sand.

'It's me who should apologise,' I said finally. 'I'd no right to get angry with you. It was a reasonable question. Just one that I don't wish to answer.'

'Fair enough,' Bill said mildly.

'I'm rather hungry,' I said, changing the subject. 'Is it a nice teashop?'

He grinned. 'They do have a very large chocolate cake on display. Sarah and I went past the place on the way to the shops. Shall we sample some?'

'That's a very good idea.'

The windows of the teashop were steamed up. A breeze had got up and made me shiver. There was a dampness which threatened rain showers. Inside was warm and stuffy and full of people. We slid politely between the tiny tables until we reached our own group. Mr Joseph, Mrs Smith and Mrs Pearson's table held a three-tiered cake stand and a teapot and cups and saucers. It was obvious they'd been there a while. Gracie waved. She and Janet had a table for two. Beside them, at the next table, sat Sarah.

'What took you so long?' she said coolly. 'I ordered for myself. You'll have to order separately.'

'That's quite fine, we shall do so,' Bill said merrily, oblivious to her mood.

We sat at the table with her. She didn't dare to shun me, but kept her attention only on Bill. He showed her the seashells. She drew back and didn't touch them.

'They're dirty. Do put them away.'

He shrugged good-naturedly and slipped them back into his pocket. The waitress arrived and we ordered a pot of tea and two slices of chocolate cake. Sarah's lemon cake was put in front of her, and another pot of tea for one.

'Let me go and bring Adam to the table,' I said. I was feeling guilty for leaving him. I didn't want trouble between us. I regretted our argument.

I hurried from the teashop and went back to the charabanc. At first I didn't see him. Then I noticed the tips of his shoes above the side of it. I clambered up onto the step. He was stretched out, dozing, on a bench. He didn't seem to notice, or mind, the light drizzling rain falling onto him.

'Adam?'

He didn't move.

'Adam?' I tried again.

He blinked and turned his head to me.

'Will you come to the teashop? It's warm in there. There's lovely chocolate cake and hot tea.'

'No. I don't care for chocolate. I'm content right here.'

'Adam . . . '

'What?'

'It doesn't matter.' I gave up and went back to join the others. I couldn't force him to be happy or to like the things that I did. Looking back now, I think I still believed then that we were right for each other. Even though the damage was already done.

My chocolate cake slice had arrived. Sarah poured the tea graciously. I tried to eat slowly. There was no conversation while we enjoyed our treat. The two ladies I'd seen on the beach came in. The little dog was left outside. They sat at the table nearest the door. I realised they weren't gentry after all, just ordinary folk; their dialect gave them away. Now that I saw them closer, their bonnets and dresses weren't fine enough to be rich.

I wondered if I'd be like them when I got older. I imagined how nice it'd be to walk along the beach every day with my pet dog, picking up shells and breathing the fresh, tangy air. But when I tried to imagine a companion, it wasn't Adam who came to mind. It was a different kind of man. One who laughed and chatted with me and shared my joy in the shells and the seals. I glanced at Bill.

He was politely offering Sarah more

tea. Mrs Pearson leaned over to ask him something. Whatever he answered, it make her chuckle so much her hat quivered. I found myself smiling. Being here, with the other servants, felt like family.

12

A Murderer Caught

I was restless. I didn't know why. We'd had a lovely day at the seaside, but that was a week past. The Dawtons were away and the house felt empty. Mrs Smith was firm that cleaning and tidying must still go on. In fact, according to the housekeeper, it was even more important, with the family in Glasgow, that we should deep-cleanse the rugs and the floors and the insides of cupboards while they weren't there to be disturbed.

Gracie and I went upstairs, lugging buckets of hot, soapy water and scrubbing brushes. We carefully peeled back the heavy rug from the upstairs living room. Then we set to work. Half an hour later, my brow was damp with sweat. Gracie had stoked up the fire earlier, knowing we'd be working here. Strictly, we weren't meant to. But Mrs Dawton wasn't here to complain.

'This is exhausting,' Gracie cried, putting down her scrubbing brush.

'It really is,' I agreed.

'Oh, I wish we were back at the seaside,' Gracie said dreamily. She pushed back her cap and wiped her face.

'Wouldn't that be nice,' I said, nodding. 'I can't settle down somehow, since we were there. It's as if there's nothing to look forward to.'

'I know just what you mean. Apart from our half-days off there's nothing to get excited about. And I don't even enjoy my day off. Mum's always on at me to get another job.'

'Because of Ellen?'

'Yes, that and the trouble with May Litton, even though it turned out that had nothing to do with it. She's heard that Mr Sankey is around Muirfield a lot, and that's spooked her too. She doesn't like me being here.'

'I thought she'd changed her mind about that?'

'So did I,' Gracie sighed. 'So did I.'

'There's not much you can do about it in any case. I've not heard of other jobs coming up.'

'Not around here, that's for sure. Well, maybe something will turn up.'

'You'd leave?' I said, dismayed.

She sighed again, unhappily. 'I don't want to, Hannah. I like it here, especially now I've got you as a friend. But I'm fed up with Mum bending my ear about it. It's wearing me down. It'd be different if they caught the murderer.'

'I don't think they will. Not now.'

She frowned at me. 'That's a change of tune from you. Not so long ago, you were going to catch him single-handedly by walking in the woods at night.'

I lifted up my hands helplessly. 'The days and weeks are flashing by, but nothing's changed. No one's acting suspiciously. Arthur Sankey is making no progress.'

'You can't say that no one's acting suspiciously,' Gracie argued. 'What about the person who pushed you?'

'I'm beginning to wonder if I imagined it all. Did I get pushed? Or did I stumble on a root and simply fall? It's possible my imagination was overwrought.'

'Really?'

I nodded. 'I think so. I got caught up in the whole thing and I thought someone was there, following me. But now I'm not sure. It's easy, in the darkness, to get a bit carried away.'

Gracie blew out a breath between pursed lips. 'So it was all for nothing?'

'I think so. Who did I think I was, setting myself up as a detective? It was silliness, plain and simple. I'm just a housemaid. Well, housemaid and lowly kitchen maid. I'm not clever, I don't have an education. Why could I work it out when a real detective couldn't?'

I was getting quite carried away in my misery and self-condemnation. Gracie half-heartedly scrubbed at a bit of floor we'd missed. Then she put down the brush once more. She knelt there and contemplated the damp wooden floor.

'Do you feel the atmosphere at Muirfield lately? Like everyone's on edge.'

'Yes, Mr Joseph was quite snappy with Mrs Pearson earlier when she wanted a couple of bottles of beer for her stew. Mrs Smith seems tense too. She was complaining of a headache, which is unlike her.'

'And Sarah's in a foul mood,' Gracie said. 'That's down to Bill.'

'Why's it Bill's fault?' I scrubbed the floor in front of me, concentrating on the grain and whorl of the wood.

'Didn't you hear? She wanted to get back together and was bold enough to suggest it. He told her no.'

Now why that should lift up my heart and make it sing, I didn't know.

'Doesn't sound like Bill, to be rude like that,' I said.

'Oh, no, he wasn't rude,' Gracie said with a firm shake of her head. 'I overheard them. He was very polite, but it was clear he meant it. Your name came up.'

'What?' I was surprised.

'Sarah blamed you for his attitude. Said that ever since you arrived, he's been distant towards her.'

'That's rubbish,' I said hotly. 'It's got nothing to do with me. Bill and I are friends, that's all.'

'I know that. Sarah was using whatever ammunition came to hand. Don't worry about it. Bill knows you're sweet on Adam.'

We finished cleaning the floor in silence. Then we took the buckets of grey water downstairs and emptied them. Mrs Smith told us to take fresh water back up and clean out the insides of the cupboards but not to leave any wetness. There were books and papers and other items, and they were to be taken out with great care and then returned to their place without breakage. Once we had our marching orders, we did as we were told.

'She's in a bad mood,' Gracie

observed, puffing her way up the steps with the heavy bucket.

'It's her headache, poor Mrs Smith. I suppose it's making her snappy.'

'She doesn't have to take it out on us,' Gracie grumbled.

We decided to begin in Mr Dawton's study. Usually it was hard to get time to clean in here, as the master used the room so much. There were a good number of cupboards to clear. With an inward sigh, I began to work.

It was nearing mid-morning when I made a discovery. I had turned out a shallow drawer in the study desk. The other drawers were locked; I supposed they held Mr Dawton's important documents. This drawer, however, was unlocked. Inside were a few general items. A pen and a bottle of ink. A blank book of paper. A map that was worn around the edges as if well-thumbed. I was glad there were few items. It meant the drawer was easy to empty and easy to return to good order.

I drew clean water onto my cloth and

wrung it out so as not to soak the inside of the drawer. All I wanted to do was take away the dust and particles within. All went well. I dried the wood with another clean cloth and carefully put the items back inside. Then I had the job of replacing the drawer into the desk.

With some adjustments, I managed to put it on the runners and began to push it gently into place. Then something brushed the top of my hand. A rough edge on the underside of the desk, where the drawer fitted. I felt for it, thinking it needed mending. Instead a piece of red wax fell into my fingers, along with a key.

It was a good place to hide a key. No one was going to find it there, unless a maid was asked to clean every nook and cranny of the desk. I took the key to Mrs Smith, knowing it was impossible to get it to stick to the desk again without fresh wax.

'You did the right thing,' the housekeeper said, taking the key from me. 'Don't worry about it. I'll ask Mr Joseph to stick it back in the desk. Mr Dawton doesn't need to know it was found.'

'Thank you, Mrs Smith,' I said gratefully. It had been an accident, after all.

It's funny how the brain works. I carried on with my tasks, enjoying Gracie's chatter and jokes. It was a good hour later before it struck me. And, like tumbling dominoes, everything fell into place.

I sat frozen like a statue, thinking about it. And then I knew exactly what I had to do.

* * *

There was no bright moonlight that night. I stood at the foot of Gracie's bed, hesitating. I wore my day clothes. My warmest dress and my coat, buttoned up tight. My stockings and boots. My bonnet. I was ready. Almost. I needed only a lantern, which I knew was in the kitchen.

'I'm sorry,' I whispered to my sleeping friend. 'I promised you not to go out in the night. But I have to. It's all changed now. Sleep well.'

Then, quietly, I closed the attic door behind me and went downstairs. It was black as night inside. I felt my way by familiarity and made it to the kitchen. There, I sought and found the lantern that Mrs Pearson kept by the door. There was a goodly sized stub of candle in it. I took matches and lit it with a shaking hand.

Then I was ready. My chest ached with tension. Nevertheless, I drew open the door and stepped out into the icy black night. The air tasted of the oncoming winter. A tendril of hair escaped and wisped my cheek. I tucked it back. I had to be able to see.

I followed the now familiar route. The horses made only small sounds, as if daunted by the night. I paused near the bothy, then went on. The woods seemed to suck in all light. I prayed my lantern would stay lit. I had extra matches in my pocket, but I didn't want to crouch somewhere in the blackness trying to relight it.

Nothing moved in the woods. There were no birds on the wing, no clip of deer's hooves, not even the creak of branches. There was no wind, just an eerie stillness. I smelt the comforting stink of the burning wax. The candle flickered but stayed lit.

'On I must go,' I whispered to myself. 'Come along, Hannah Miller. You can do this.'

And so to the inevitable sight of the summerhouse. The lake was almost invisible, a wide inky blot behind the wooden building. The trees beyond melded in darkness with the night sky. It was hard to find my bearings. The path under my soles was my only guide.

I stumbled slightly on reaching the wooden platform. I put out my hand to save me tripping. The wood was rough and my fingertips tingled. A splinter dug into my skin. I drew it out blindly. Setting the lantern down, I checked my hands by its low yellow light. They were sore, but that was all. No injuries, thank goodness.

I lifted up the lantern and pushed open the door to the summerhouse. It was as empty as always. Yet now I knew it held a secret; I was certain of it. Without further ado, I knelt down and opened up the cupboards under the seating.

The lantern shone inside. The cupboards were empty, just as before. But now my quick fingers felt the underside of the seating, which formed the ceiling of the cupboards. And almost immediately I found what I was looking for.

I felt paper and wax under my fingers. I pulled the packages down and brought them out. I hadn't even opened the first one when the door creaked open.

Hadn't I expected this? Didn't I know, in my heart, that he'd come? Yet it felt as if that very same heart was now breaking. I hadn't wanted it to be true.

'How did you find out?'

I turned to face him, the packages

clutched in my fingers. Adam, my sweet Adam. He stood there, tall and broad-shouldered, a black silhouette I could barely see.

'I didn't know for sure. I guessed.' My voice was surprisingly steady. It was as if we were holding a normal conversation.

'I deserve what's in those packets. More than he does.' Adam's voice was thick with emotion. 'That's my future. I'll be head gardener in a grand estate in England on the back of those. Mr Dawton doesn't know the worth of what he's got.'

'You're selling his precious plant seeds without his knowledge.' My guess had been correct.

'You'd be amazed what growers will pay for what's in there,' Adam said. 'Some of those seeds are so rare there's only one or two plants growing in this entire country. If I sell them to the right people, rich men, then they'll need someone knowledgeable to grow them on. I've got buyers lined up in London.

That's where I'm headed.'

'It's stealing. If Mr Dawton found out, he'd sack you. You'd lose everything — your reputation and any chance of good future employment. It would all be over. Ellen found out about this, didn't she?'

'She wouldn't stop about it. She threatened me. Said she'd tell Mr Dawton if I didn't marry her and share the wealth.'

'Why not marry her then? Was it such an awful idea?' Poor Ellen. She'd sadly misjudged her threats. She must have believed Adam loved her enough.

'I couldn't have a wife I didn't trust. She'd have given me up any time I didn't agree with her.'

He took a step forward. I took an equal step back. I held the lantern in front of me as if it was a barrier.

'I didn't want to get rid of her. She went on and on. It was an accident.' He covered his face with his hands and groaned.

'What about me? Will I be an

accident too?' I whispered to his bent head. 'Did you love me at all?'

He paused and then slowly raised his head. For a moment our gazes met. It was too dark for me to see the beauty of his blue eyes, but I felt a pang like a physical blow for all that could have been. I had loved this man. But I had never really known him. I'd been a fool. I'd been taken in by his handsome features and strong body. The real Adam was something quite different.

'I don't know what to do,' he said. His voice was sad and regretful.

The tiny hairs on the back of my neck prickled. 'I'm going to go straight to the house and get them to call Arthur Sankey. I can't pretend that I won't,' I said.

He moved forward. At that moment the door crashed open and Bill came running in. He tackled Adam to the ground. In the commotion the lantern was knocked over and went out. There was a scuffling and kicking. I screamed. I didn't know which man was which. A flying foot caught me on the shin. I cried out and fell back.

When the chaos stopped, Adam was lying face down on the ground with his hands tied behind his back. Bill was standing, breathing heavily. Behind him, timidly peering, was Miss Emily. I sat, somewhat stunned, my bonnet choking my neck with its ribbons. I loosened it and threw it off.

Bill ran to me. 'Hannah, are you hurt? Did he touch you?' His fingers ran round my face and head, searching for wounds. With a sigh of relief, he moved away. 'You've Miss Emily to thank for your rescue. She came and woke me up, insisted we go to the summerhouse. She was watching you leave. She knows that Adam killed Ellen.'

'Why didn't she say so before?' I looked from Bill to Emily and back again, puzzled.

'I thought I was asleep,' Emily piped up now. She came and sat beside me. We both looked at the bound man on the floor. He made no movement or sound. Bill was taking no chances. He looked ready for action, if Adam made any threat.

'I was sleepwalking, as I do. I found myself here when I woke up. I heard angry voices, so I hid in the trees. Then I saw . . . him and the maid. It was horrible. I heard the splash of water, and then she wasn't there anymore, only him. I stayed hidden until he'd gone. Afterwards, I thought it was a nightmare, not real.'

'And when you saw me tonight?' I prompted gently, putting my arm around her.

'I saw you with the lantern. Somehow I knew it was bad. I like Bill. He's kind to me. And he likes you; I've seen how he looks at you. I knew he'd help save you.'

She snuggled into my arms and stayed there. Her hair was soft under my chin. I felt a surge of protectiveness for this child who had helped save me. I looked up at Bill. 'You did save me. Thank you.'

He coughed with embarrassment and nodded. We both pretended not to have heard Emily's words about how much Bill liked me.

'Now we have to go and rouse Arthur Sankey to come and arrest Adam.'

★   ★   ★

After it was all done and Adam had been taken away, we sat in the kitchen. The whole household was up. Mrs Pearson, wrapped in her dressing gown and with her hair hanging in a long grey plait, made cups of hot chocolate for everybody. Emily wouldn't leave my side. She nibbled on a ginger biscuit and took gulps of her hot chocolate as if she couldn't quite believe she was having a midnight feast. Mrs Smith got Janet to stoke up the fire so that it was quite warm. Mr Joseph, complete with his pointed nightcap, sat looking bewildered. Gracie looked simply cross. I didn't blame her. I had some explaining to do. I'd broken my promise to her. It had very nearly ended badly.

I was suddenly and completely so very glad that it was none of them that was the culprit. They had all become so dear to me. Even Mr Joseph, despite his petty crimes. I realised I had to have a quiet word with him about that. But it could wait until the morning.

'How did you know it was Adam?' Bill asked.

Everyone leaned in to hear what I had to say. It was rather unnerving. I paused to take a comforting sip of my drink before speaking.

'It wasn't until I found Mr Dawton's key that everything fell into place.' Then of course I had to explain about the key in the wax before going on. 'I had gathered from what Mr Dawton said about his plant collections that they were worth a lot of money. And from Adam, I learned that they were difficult to grow and therefore some of them were extremely rare. I found myself wondering what someone might do with that information, especially a man who was as driven by ambition as Adam. He appeared, sadly, to have the strongest motive out of all of you for keeping Ellen silent if she found out his secrets.

'I couldn't work out where he stored the seeds out of sight of Mr Dawton, or Mr Crickett and Peter. I was drawn to the summerhouse. Adam had given me a flower there as if the place had a significance for him. I searched the cupboards, but there was nothing. Then when I found the key, I realised the same method could be used in the summerhouse too. Adam must have seen the lantern as I passed. You all know what happened then.'

I stopped there. To my embarrassment, tears poured down my face and I cried. Bill rushed to my side to hug me. Mrs Smith opened her mouth to say something but shut it again and smiled.

13

Spring Wedding

Bill and I were married in the spring. The wedding took place in the church in my village where generations of my foremothers had walked down the aisle. Our families and friends were all there to see us wed before we returned to the cottage for a late wedding breakfast. The neighbours had been very generous, helping with dishes of food. Mam's ex-employer had sent a hamper with gorgeous hams and cheeses, and the Dawtons too had sent enough for a fine feast.

'Well, it's them that paid for it, but me that prepared it,' Mrs Pearson said, puffing along the lane back to the cottage.

'Thank you, Mrs Pearson. It's very much appreciated by my husband and me,' I said, Bill tall and proud by my side. I enjoyed rolling the word 'husband' around in my mouth. Savouring it. It turned out that I was very much in love with Bill. My feelings for Adam were a pale, washed-out emotion by comparison. Bill argued that he'd loved me first. He'd loved me the moment I bumped into him on my first day at Muirfield Hall. I told him he'd a fine way of showing it, being a grumpy sort who never spoke to me. He said to forget all that and enjoy what we had now. Being an excellent sort of wife, I had to agree.

'Looks like I'll be preparing food for another wedding before long,' the cook said with a jerk of her head behind us.

Gracie and Johnny were walking along, heads together and talking. She caught me looking and threw me a very happy smile. I was sure Mrs Pearson was right. I was very glad for her. Gracie had forgiven me eventually for breaking my promise. But it had taken weeks to get back into her good books.

She said the pain of nearly losing me was too much to bear. It might have been heroic to tackle Adam that way, but it was also incredibly foolish. I knew she was right. I had been very, very lucky the way things turned out.

Mam and Dad came along the lane more slowly. He was looking better than in previous months, and I hoped he'd continue to improve. The happiness my marriage had brought to our family seemed to have boosted his health.

It was a dry day, luckily, because we wouldn't have fitted everyone under the cottage roof. From somewhere trestle tables had appeared. Mrs Pearson, with Gracie and Janet's help, loaded them up with crisp white tablecloths and mountains of food and drink. Mr Joseph poured out wine. He had given up his idea of being head butler at the grand house beyond Muirfield. After our little chat, he'd realised just how lucky he was to be butler there. I never referred to our conversation again. I heard from Kitty, courtesy of her strange, long string of a grapevine that all his dealings had stopped. He became a model butler, and I think he was happier too. Instead of always wishing to be somewhere else, he made Muirfield his project and worked hard for the Dawtons.

'Did you not invite your aunt?' Mrs Smith said, holding a plate of ham and a small glass of wine.

'My aunt?' I said, puzzled.

'Yes, the aunt you visited in the market town last year.'

'Oh . . . ' I tried for an answer and failed. It seemed shabby now to continue with such a fabrication. I was ashamed enough of having lied to her.

'I expect she didn't wish to come. I recall you said she liked to keep herself to herself.' There was a twinkle in Mrs Smith's eyes before she left me to join Mrs Pearson.

I wondered when she'd guessed. The story of my detective work had intrigued the other servants when it all came out. Naturally some of it had to remain secret. I didn't mention Mr Joseph's part in it, for example. And I had certainly never talked about following Mrs Smith. It would have been terribly unkind to tell everyone where her brother was.

I picked some choice morsels for my own plate. Bill was laughing with Johnny and Gracie. Mam and Kitty were standing together. Dad had taken a seat and was enjoying watching the party. I stared out across the fields. There were splashes of yellow where coltsfoot and lesser celandine flowered, and the hawthorn buds were a vivid, bright green. There was hope in the air.

'Do you ever think about him?' Bill's voice said in my ear.

'No.' I shook my head firmly.

It was true. I had shut Adam's fate from my mind. I wanted only to look to the future. There was a new gardener at Muirfield now. Mr Dawton boasted that he could raise the most tender of plants. Mr Crickett had muttered about retiring. Peter told me he wasn't interested in the position of head gardener. He liked pottering about and didn't want the responsibility. It looked as if either the new man would rise high quickly or someone else might be brought in. Things changed, I mused. Even if you liked them the way they were. Nothing stayed forever.

Bill took my hand and led me back to our wedding celebration. It was a day to be jolly, not sad.

Sarah was beautiful in a green silk dress. I knew it was a cast-off from Mrs Dawton, but it fitted her slender frame very well. Her glorious hair was loose. She came up to me when Bill was called away by my father for a chat.

'Congratulations.'

'Thank you,' I said warily.

'Can we be friends?' Sarah said. 'Can we start afresh? I know I haven't acted well towards you.'

I was very pleased and surprised. Impulsively, I hugged her. For a moment she stiffened, then she returned the pressure of my arms.

'I'd like that very much,' I said.

She flushed almost as red as her hair. 'You see, for a long while I fancied myself in love with Bill. I disliked you for taking him away.'

'I didn't try to take him away,' I defended myself.

'I know, but that's how it seemed to me. Anyway, I've fallen in love with Ian up at the estate beyond Muirfield. He's a good match for me. We've plans to emigrate to America. It's a land of opportunity for young people who want to work hard.'

'I wish you all the best, I really do,' I said. 'And I'm glad we're friends.'

* * *

Bill and I left Muirfield too. In a way I was sad to do so, yet the place held memories that disturbed me. We had an opportunity to manage a shop in the seaside village where we'd had the day out. And so I got my wish to visit there in the spring and summer. In fact we were able to observe and enjoy the seaside in all its seasons and weathers. I amassed a fine collection of seashells, driftwood and other treasures. We never tired of taking walks along the sands together.

Gracie and Johnny got married and worked for some years on a farm near his folks. When we bought the shop, they came to help run the business. Soon we expanded to buying the teashop too, and there was enough work to keep us all active and interested the rest of our lives.

In time, Bill and I had three children to help in the shops and to leave our businesses to. We were often over to visit with my parents and Kitty, who was a fine and proud aunt. Bill, having no family of his own, was in his element as a son-in-law and as a father.

The Dawtons had sold up at Muirfield shortly after we moved to the seaside. Mrs Dawton had found a large townhouse in an exclusive part of Glasgow. Mr Dawton didn't fight the move, according to Mrs Smith, who often wrote to me. The new couple who bought Muirfield didn't care for gardening. The last I heard, the walled gardens had gone to ruins, with brambles and willows growing wild; and the strange and exotic plants that had obsessed Adam were lost as the gardens reverted to their natural state.

We do hope that you have enjoyed reading this large print book.

Did you know that all of our titles are available for purchase?

We publish a wide range of high quality large print books including:
Romances, Mysteries, Classics
General Fiction
Non Fiction and Westerns

Special interest titles available in large print are:
The Little Oxford Dictionary
Music Book, Song Book
Hymn Book, Service Book

Also available from us courtesy of Oxford University Press:
Young Readers' Dictionary
(large print edition)
Young Readers' Thesaurus
(large print edition)

For further information or a free brochure, please contact us at:
Ulverscroft Large Print Books Ltd.,
The Green, Bradgate Road, Anstey,
Leicester, LE7 7FU, England.
Tel: (00 44) **0116 236 4325**
Fax: (00 44) **0116 234 0205**

CROSSING WITH THE CAPTAIN

Judy Jarvie

Ten years ago, Libby Grant and Drew Muldoon dated for six months. Despite a string of disasters, they became engaged — then Libby broke up by letter while Drew was at sea. Now on a leisure cruise around Spain and Italy, she discovers to her horror that Drew is the captain of the ship. Can they work through their past problems and rekindle the spark and hope of their old relationship? Or will the mysterious thefts and hacking incidents on board the ship throw a serious spanner in the works?

THE LEMON TREE

Sheila Spencer-Smith

When her boyfriend Charles suggests they spend two months apart, Zoe's brother Simon invites her to come stay with him and his wife Thea in the idyllic village of Elounda on Crete, where they run a taverna. There Zoe meets Adam, an English tour guide. But business at the taverna isn't exactly brisk, and Adam will be leaving soon. Can Zoe make things work, or will she decide to return to her old life and Charles?